ALSO BY

ELENA FERRANTE

The Days of Abandonment
Troubling Love
My Brilliant Friend
The Story of a New Name
Those Who Leave and Those Who Stay

THE LOST
DAUGHTER

Elena Ferrante

THE LOST DAUGHTER

Translated from the Italian
by Ann Goldstein

Europa
editions

Europa Editions
214 West 29th Street
New York, N.Y. 10001
www.europaeditions.com
info@europaeditions.com

Copyright © 2006 by Edizioni e/o
First Publication 2008 by Europa Editions
Sixth printing, 2015

Translation by Ann Goldstein
Original title: *La figlia oscura*
Translation copyright © 2007 by Europa Editions

Library of Congress Cataloging in Publication Data is available
ISBN 978-1-933372-42-6

Ferrante, Elena
The Lost Daughter

Book design by Emanuele Ragnisco
www.mekkanografici.com
Cover photograph © Freyda Miller/CORBIS

Prepress by Plan.ed – Rome

Printed in the USA

THE LOST
DAUGHTER

1

I had been driving for less than an hour when I began to feel ill. The burning in my side came back, but at first I decided not to give it any importance. I became worried only when I realized that I no longer had the strength to hold onto the steering wheel. In the space of a few minutes my head became heavy, the headlights grew dimmer; soon I even forgot that I was driving. I had the impression, rather, of being at the sea, in the middle of the day. The beach was empty, the water calm, but on a pole a few meters from shore a red flag was waving. When I was a child, my mother had frightened me, saying, Leda, you must never go swimming if you see a red flag: it means the sea is rough and you might drown. That fear had endured through the years, and even now, although the water was a sheet of translucent paper stretching to the horizon, I didn't dare go in: I was anxious. I said to myself, go on, swim: they must have forgotten the flag, and meanwhile I stayed on the shore, cautiously testing the water with the tip of my toe. Only at intervals my mother appeared at the top of the dunes and shouted to me as if I were still a child: Leda, what are you doing, don't you see the red flag?

In the hospital, when I opened my eyes, I saw myself again hesitating for a fraction of a second before the flat sea. Maybe that was why, later, I convinced myself that it wasn't a dream but a fantasy of alarm that lasted until I woke up in the hospital room. The doctors told me that my car had ended up against the guardrail but without critical consequences. The only serious injury was in my left side, an inexplicable lesion.

My friends from Florence came, Bianca and Marta returned, and even Gianni. I said it was drowsiness that had sent me off the road. But I knew very well that drowsiness wasn't to blame. At the origin was a gesture of mine that made no sense, and which, precisely because it was senseless, I immediately decided not to speak of to anyone. The hardest things to talk about are the ones we ourselves can't understand.

2

When my daughters moved to Toronto, where their father had lived and worked for years, I was embarrassed and amazed to discover that I wasn't upset; rather, I felt light, as if only then had I definitively brought them into the world. For the first time in almost twenty-five years I was not aware of the anxiety of having to take care of them. The house was neat, as if no one lived there, I no longer had the constant bother of shopping and doing the laundry, the woman who for years had helped with the household chores found a better-paying job and I felt no need to replace her.

My only obligation with regard to the girls was to call once a day to see how they were, what they were doing. On the phone they spoke as if they were on their own; in reality they lived with their father, but, accustomed to keeping us separate even in words, they spoke to me as if he didn't exist. To my questions on the state of their lives they answered either in a cheerfully evasive manner, or with an ill humor full of irritable pauses, or in the artificial tones they assumed when they were in the company of friends. They called me often, too, especially Bianca, who had a more imperiously demanding relationship with me, but only to know if blue shoes would go with an orange skirt, if I could find some papers left in a book and send them urgently, if I was still available to be blamed for their rages, their sorrows, in spite of the different continents and the spacious sky that separated us. The telephone calls were almost always hurried, sometimes they seemed fake, as in a movie.

I did what they asked, reacted in accordance with their expectations. But since distance imposed the physical impossibility of intervening directly in their lives, satisfying their desires or whims became a mixture of rarefied or irresponsible gestures, every request seemed light, every task that had to do with them an affectionate habit. I felt miraculously unfettered, as if a difficult job, finally brought to completion, no longer weighed me down.

I began to work without regard for their schedules and their needs. I corrected my students' papers at night, listening to music; I slept a lot in the afternoon, with earplugs; I ate once a day and always at a trattoria next door. I changed rapidly—my habits, my mood, my very physical appearance. At the university I was no longer irritated by the students who were too stupid and those who were too smart. A colleague I had known for years and whom occasionally, rarely, I slept with, said to me in bewilderment one evening that I had become less distracted, more generous. In a few months I regained the slender body of my youth and felt a sensation of gentle strength; it seemed to me that my thoughts had returned to their proper speed. One night I looked at myself in the mirror. I was forty-seven years old, I would be forty-eight in four months, but by some magic years had fallen from me. I don't know if I was pleased; certainly I was surprised.

It was in this state of unusual well-being that, when June came, I felt like taking a vacation, and I decided that I would go to the sea as soon as I had finished with exams and the annoying bureaucratic formalities. I looked on the Internet, studied photographs and prices. Finally I rented a small, fairly inexpensive apartment on the Ionian coast, from mid-July to the end of August. In fact, I didn't manage to leave until July 24th. The drive was easy, the car packed mainly with books that I needed for preparing next year's courses. The day was beautiful; through the open windows came a breeze full of parched summer scents, and I felt free and without guilt at my freedom.

But halfway there, as I was getting gas, I felt suddenly anxious. In the past I had loved the sea, but for at least fifteen years being in the sun had made me nervous, exhausted me instantly. The apartment would surely be ugly, the view a distant slice of blue amid cheap, squalid houses. I wouldn't sleep a wink because of the heat and some night club playing music at high volume. I made the rest of the journey with a faint ill humor and the sense that I would have been able to work at home comfortably all summer, breathing the air-conditioned air in the silence of my apartment.

When I arrived the sun was setting. The town seemed pretty, the voices had a pleasing cadence, there were good smells. Waiting for me was an old man with thick white hair who was respectfully cordial. First he bought me a coffee at the bar, and then, with a mixture of smiles and unmistakable gestures, he prevented me from carrying even a single bag into the house. Loaded down with my suitcases, he climbed, panting, to the fourth and top floor, and put them down in the doorway of a small penthouse: bedroom, tiny windowless kitchen that opened directly into the bathroom, a living room with big picture windows, and a terrace from which one could see, in the twilight, a rocky, jagged coast and an infinite sea.

The man's name was Giovanni; he wasn't the owner of the apartment but a sort of caretaker or handyman; yet he wouldn't accept a tip, in fact, he was almost offended, as if I hadn't understood that he was merely following the rules of a proper welcome. When, having been assured many times that everything was to my satisfaction, he left, I found on the table in the living room a big tray of peaches, plums, pears, grapes, and figs. The tray shone as if in a still-life.

I carried a wicker chair out to the terrace, and sat for a while to watch the evening descend on the sea. For years every vacation had revolved around the two children, and when they got older and began traveling the world with their friends I always stayed home, waiting for their return. I worried not only about all kinds of catastrophes (the dangers of air travel, ocean voyages, wars, earthquakes, tidal waves) but about their fragile nervous systems, possible tensions with their traveling companions, sentimental dramas because of affections returned too easily or not returned at all. I wanted to be ready to cope with sudden requests for help, I was afraid they would accuse me of being what in fact I was, distracted or absent, absorbed in myself. Enough. I got up, went to take a shower.

Afterward I was hungry and went back to the tray of fruit. I discovered that under the beautiful show figs, pears, prunes, peaches, grapes were overripe or rotten. I took a knife and cut off large black areas, but the smell disgusted me, the taste, and I threw almost all of it in the garbage. I could go out, look for a restaurant, but I gave up on eating because I was tired, I wanted to sleep.

In the bedroom there were two large windows. I opened them and turned off the lights. Outside, every so often, I saw the beam of a lighthouse explode out of the darkness and strike the room for a few seconds. One should never arrive in an unknown place at night, everything is undefined, every object is easily exaggerated. I lay down on the bed in my bathrobe, my hair wet, and stared at the ceiling, waiting for the moment when it would become white with light. I heard the distant sound of an outboard motor and a faint song that was like a meow. I had no contours. I turned drowsily and touched something on the pillow that felt cold, something made of tissue paper.

I turned on the light. On the bright-white material of the pillowcase was an insect, three or four centimeters long, like a giant fly. It was dark brown, and motionless, with membranous wings. I said to myself: it's a cicada, maybe its abdomen burst on my pillow. I touched it with the hem of my bathrobe, it moved and became immediately quiet. Male, female. The stomach of the females doesn't have elastic membranes, it doesn't sing, it's mute. I felt disgust. The cicada punctures olive trees and makes the sap drip from the bark of the mountain ash. I cautiously picked up the pillow, went to one of the windows, and tossed the insect out. That was how my vacation began.

3

The next day I put in my bag bathing suit, beach towels, books, xeroxes, notebooks, got in the car, and went in search of beach and sea along the county road that followed the coast. After about twenty minutes a pinewood appeared on my right. I saw a sign for parking, and stopped. Loaded down with my things, I climbed over the guardrail and set off along a path reddened by pine needles.

I love the scent of resin: as a child, I spent summers on beaches not yet completely eaten away by the concrete of the Camorra—they began where the pinewood ended. That scent was the scent of vacation, of the summer games of childhood. The squeak or thud of a dry pinecone, the dark color of the pine nuts reminds me of my mother's mouth: she laughs as she crushes the shells, takes out the yellow fruit, gives it to my sisters, noisy and demanding, or to me, waiting in silent expectation, or eats it herself, staining her lips with dark powder and saying, to teach me not to be so timid: go on, none for you, you're worse than a green pinecone.

The pinewood was very thick, with a tangled undergrowth, and the trunks, which had grown up bending under the force of the wind, seemed on the point of falling over, fearful of something that came from the sea. I took care not to stumble on the shiny roots that crisscrossed the path and controlled my revulsion at the dusty lizards that left the patches of sun as I passed and fled in search of shelter. I walked for no more than five minutes, then the dunes and the sea appeared. I passed the twisted trunks of eucalyptus growing out of the sand, took a wooden walkway among green reeds and oleanders, and came to a tidy public bath house.

I liked the place immediately. I was reassured by the kindness of the dark man at the counter, by the gentle young beach attendant, who, tall and thin, unmuscular, in a T-shirt and red shorts, led me to an umbrella. The sand was white powder, I took a long swim in transparent water, and sat in the sun. Then I settled myself in the shade with my books and worked in peace until sunset, enjoying the breeze and the rapid changes of the sea. The hours slipped away in such a gentle mixture of work, daydreams, and idleness that I decided I would keep going back there.

In less than a week it had all become a peaceful routine. I liked the squeak of the pinecones opening to the sun as I cross the pinewood, the scent of small green leaves that seemed to be myrtle, the strips of bark peeling off the eucalyptus trees. On the path I imagined winter, the pinewood frozen among the fogs, the broom that produced red berries. Every day on my arrival the man at the counter greeted me with polite satisfaction; I had a coffee at the bar, a glass of water. The attendant, whose name was Gino and who was surely a student, promptly opened the umbrella and the lounge chair, and then withdrew into the shade, his full lips parted, his eyes intent as he underlined with a pencil the pages of a big volume for some exam or other.

I felt tender as I looked at that boy. Usually I dozed as I dried off in the sun, but sometimes I didn't sleep; eyes half closed, I observed him with sympathy, taking care that he wouldn't notice. He seemed restless, contorting his handsome, nervous body, running the fingers of one hand through his glossy black hair, worrying his chin. My daughters would have liked him, especially Marta, who fell in love easily with lean, nervous boys. As for me, who knows. I realized long ago that I've held onto little of myself and everything of them. Even now, I was looking at Gino through the filter of Bianca's experiences, of Marta's, according to the tastes and passions I imagine as theirs.

The young man was studying, but he seemed to have sensors independent of sight. If I merely made a move to shift the lounge chair from the sun to the shade, he would jump up, ask if I needed help. I smiled, shook my head no, what did it take to move a lounge chair. It was enough to feel myself protected, without deadlines to keep in mind, nothing urgent to confront. No one depended anymore on my care and, finally, even I was no longer a burden to myself.

4

The young mother and her daughter I became aware of later. I don't know if they had been there since my first day on the beach or appeared afterward. In the three or four days following my arrival I hardly noticed a rather loud group of Neapolitans, children, adults, a man in his sixties with a mean expression, four or five children who fought fiercely in the water and on land, a large woman with short legs and heavy breasts, nearly forty, perhaps, who went back and forth between the beach and the bar, painfully dragging a pregnant belly, the great, naked arc stretched between the two halves of her bathing suit. They were all related, parents, grandparents, children, grandchildren, cousins, in-laws, and their laughter rang out noisily. They called each other by name with drawn-out cries, hurled exclamatory or conspiratorial comments, at times quarreled: a large family group, similar to the one I had been part of when I was a girl, the same jokes, the same sentimentality, the same rages.

One day I looked up from my book and, for the first time, saw the young woman and the little girl. They were returning from the water's edge to their umbrella, she no more than twenty, her head bent, and the child, three or four years old, gazing up at her, rapt, holding a doll the way a mother carries a child in her arms. They were talking to each other peacefully, as if they alone existed. From the umbrella, the pregnant woman called out irritatedly in their direction, and a fat gray-haired woman in her fifties, fully dressed, who was perhaps the mother, made gestures of discontent, disapproving of I don't know what. But the girl seemed deaf and blind, she went on talking to the child and walking up from the sea with measured steps, leaving on the sand the dark shadow of her footprints.

They, too, were part of the big noisy family, but she, the young mother, seen this way, from a distance, with her slim body, the tastefully chosen one-piece bathing suit, the slender neck, the shapely head and long, wavy, glossy black hair, the Indian face with its high cheekbones, the heavy eyebrows and slanting eyes, seemed to me an anomaly in the group, an organism that had mysteriously escaped the rule, the victim, now assimilated, of a kidnapping or of an exchange in the cradle.

I got into the habit of looking every so often in their direction.

There was something off about the little girl, I don't know what; a childish sadness, perhaps, or a silent illness.

Her whole face expressed a permanent request to her mother that they stay together: it was an entreaty without tears or tantrums, which the mother did not evade. Once I noticed the tenderness with which she rubbed lotion on her. And once I was struck by the leisurely time that mother and daughter spent in the water together, the mother hugging the child to her, the child with her arms tight around the mother's neck. They laughed together, enjoying the feeling of body against body, touching noses, spitting out streams of water, kissing each other. On one occasion I saw them playing with the doll. They did it with such pleasure, dressing her, undressing her, pretending to put suntan lotion on her; they bathed her in a green pail, they dried her, rubbing her so that she wouldn't catch cold, hugged her to their breast as if to nurse her, or fed her baby food of sand; they kept her in the sun with them, lying on their towel. If the young woman was pretty herself, in her motherhood there was something that distinguished her; she seemed to have no desire for anything but her child.

Not that she wasn't well integrated into the big family group. She talked endlessly to the pregnant woman, played cards with some sunburned youths of her own age, cousins, I think, walked along the shore with the fierce-looking old man (her father?), or with the boisterous young women, sisters, cousins, sisters-in-law. It didn't seem to me that she had a husband or someone who was obviously the father of the child. I noted instead that all the members of the family took affectionate care of her and the child. The gray, fat woman in her fifties accompanied her to the bar to buy ice cream for the little girl. The children, at her sharp cry, interrupted their squabbling and, though they grumbled, went to get water, food, whatever she needed. As soon as mother and daughter went out a little way from the shore in a small red-and-blue rowboat, the pregnant woman cried Nina, Lenù, Ninetta, Lena, and hurried breathlessly to the water's edge, alarming even the attendant, who jumped to his feet, to keep an eye on the situation. Once when the girl was approached by two young men who wanted to start a conversation, the cousins immediately intervened, with shoving and rude words, nearly provoking a fistfight.

For a while I didn't know if it was the mother or the daughter who was called Nina, Ninù, Ninè, the names were so many, and I had trouble, given the thick weave of sound, arriving at any conclusion. Then, by listening to voices and cries, I realized that Nina was the mother. It was more complicated with the child, and in the beginning I was confused. I thought she had a nickname like Nani or Nena or Nennella, but then I understood that those were the names of the doll, from whom the child was never parted and to whom Nina paid attention as if she were alive, a second daughter. The child in reality was called Elena, Lenù; the mother always called her Elena, the relatives Lenù.

I don't know why, I wrote those names in my notebook, Elena, Nani, Nena, Leni; maybe I liked the way Nina pronounced them. She talked to the child and her doll in the pleasing cadence of the Neapolitan dialect that I love, the tender language of playfulness and sweet nothings. I was enchanted. Languages for me have a secret venom that every so often foams up and for which there is no antidote. I remember the dialect on my mother's lips when she lost that gentle cadence and yelled at us, poisoned by her unhappiness: I can't take you anymore, I can't take any more. Commands, shouts, insults, life stretching into her words, as when a frayed nerve is just touched, and the pain scrapes away all self-control. Once, twice, three times she threatened us, her daughters, that she would leave, you'll wake up in the morning and won't find me here. And every morning I woke trembling with fear. In reality she was always there, in her words she was constantly disappearing from home. That woman, Nina, seemed serene, and I felt envious.

5

Nearly a week of vacation had already slipped away: good weather, a light breeze, a lot of empty umbrellas, cadences of dialects from all over Italy mixed with the local dialect and the languages of a few foreigners who had come for the sun.

Then it was Saturday, and the beach grew crowded. My patch of sun and shade was besieged by coolers, pails, shovels, plastic water wings and floats, racquets. I gave up reading and searched the crowd for Nina and Elena as if they were a show, to help pass the time.

I had a hard time finding them; I saw that they had dragged their lounge chair closer to the water. Nina was lying on her stomach, in the sun, and beside her, in the same position, it seemed to me, was the doll. The child, on the other hand, had gone to the water's edge with a yellow plastic watering can, filled it with water, and, holding it with both hands because of the weight, puffing and laughing, returned to her mother to water her body and mitigate

the sun's heat. When the watering can was empty, she went
to fill it again, same route, same effort, same game.

Maybe I had slept badly, maybe some unpleasant
thought had passed through my head that I was unaware
of; certainly, seeing them that morning I felt irritated.
Elena, for example, seemed to me obtusely methodical:
first she watered her mother's ankles, then the doll's, she
asked both if that was enough, both said no, she went off
again. Nina, on the other hand, seemed to me affected: she
mewed with pleasure, repeated the mewing in a different
tone, as if it were coming from the doll's mouth, and then
sighed, again, again. I suspected that she was playing her
role of beautiful young mother not for love of her daughter but for us, the crowd on the beach, all of us, male and
female, young and old.

The sprinkling of her body and the doll's went on for a
long time. She became shiny with water, the luminous needles sprayed by the watering can wet her hair, too, which
stuck to her head and forehead. Nani or Nile or Nena, the
doll, was soaked with the same perseverance, but she
absorbed less water, and so it dripped from the blue plastic of the lounger onto the sand, darkening it.

I stared at the child in her coming and going and I don't
know what bothered me, the game with the water, perhaps, or Nina flaunting her pleasure in the sun. Or the
voices, yes, especially the voices that mother and daughter
attributed to the doll. Now they gave her words in turn,
now together, superimposing the adult's fake-child voice
and the child's fake-adult voice. They imagined it was the
same, single voice coming from the same throat of a thing
in reality mute. But evidently I couldn't enter into their
illusion, I felt a growing repulsion for that double voice.

Of course, there I was, at a distance, what did it matter to me, I could follow the game or ignore it, it was only a pastime. But no, I felt an unease as if faced with a thing done badly, as if a part of me were insisting, absurdly, that they should make up their minds, give the doll a stable, constant voice, either that of the mother or that of the daughter, and stop pretending that they were the same.

It was like a slight twinge that, as you keep thinking about it, becomes an unbearable pain. I was beginning to feel exasperated. At a certain point I wanted to get up, make my way obliquely over to the lounge chair where they were playing, and, stopping there, say That's enough, you don't know how to play, stop it. With that intention I even left my place, I couldn't bear it any longer. Naturally I said nothing, I went by looking straight ahead. I thought: it's too hot, I've always hated crowded places, everyone talking with the same modulated sounds, moving for the same reasons, doing the same things. I blamed the weekend beach for my sudden attack of nerves and went to stick my feet in the water.

6

Around noon something new happened. I was napping in the shade, even though the music that came from the bath house was too loud, when I heard the pregnant woman calling Nina, as if she had something extraordinary to announce.

I opened my eyes, noticed the girl pick up her daughter, and point out to her something or someone behind me with exaggerated cheerfulness. I turned and saw a heavy, thickset man, between thirty and forty, who was coming down the wooden walkway, his head completely shaved, wearing a tight-fitting black T-shirt that held in a substantial belly above green bathing trunks. The child recognized him, made signs of greeting, but nervously, laughing and coyly hiding her face between her mother's neck and shoulder. The man, with a serious expression, gave a faint wave. His face was handsome, his eyes sharp. In no hurry, he stopped to greet the manager, gave an affectionate pat to the young attendant, who had immediately come over, and at the same time an entourage of large jovial men in bathing suits also stopped, one with a backpack, one with a cooler, one with two or three packages, which, to judge from the ribbons and bows, must be gifts. When the man finally reached the beach, Nina came up to him carrying the child, again stopping the little procession. He, still serious, with composed gestures, first of all took Elena from her embrace; the child hugged him, arms around his neck, giving his cheeks small anxious kisses. Then, still offering his cheek to her, he seized Nina behind the neck, almost forcing her to bend over—he was at least four inches shorter than she was—and fleetingly touched her lips, with restrained, proprietary command.

I guessed that Elena's father had arrived, Nina's husband. Among the Neapolitans a kind of party started up immediately, and they crowded around, right up to the edge of my umbrella. I saw that the child was unwrapping presents, that Nina was trying on an ugly straw hat. Then the new arrival pointed to something on the sea, a white motorboat. The old man with the mean look, the boys, the fat gray-haired woman, the girl and boy cousins gathered along the shore, shouting and waving their arms in signs of greeting. The motorboat passed the line of red buoys, zigzagged among the swimmers, crossed the line of white buoys, and arrived, its motor still running, amid children and old people swimming in the shallow water. Heavy men with worn faces, ostentatiously wealthy women, obese children jumped out. Embraces, kisses on the cheek, Nina's hat carried it off by the wind. Her husband, like a motionless animal that at the first sign of danger springs with unexpected force and decisiveness, grabbed it in midair, despite the child in his arms, before it ended up in the water, and gave it back to her. She put it on more carefully; suddenly the hat seemed pretty, and I felt an irrational pang of unease.

The confusion grew. The new arrivals were evidently disappointed by the arrangement of the umbrellas; the husband called Gino over, and the manager came, too. I got the impression that they all wanted to be together, the resident family group and those who were visiting, forming a compact wedge of loungers and chairs and coolers, of children and adults having a good time. They pointed in my direction, where there were two free umbrellas, with a lot of gestures, especially the pregnant woman, who eventually began asking her neighbors to move, to shift from one umbrella to another, just as at the movies someone asks if you would please move over a few seats.

A game-like atmosphere was created. The bathers hesitated, they didn't want to move, with all their belongings, but both the children and the adults of the Neapolitan family were already cheerfully packing up, and finally most of the bathers moved almost willingly.

I opened a book, but by now I had a knot of bitter feelings inside that at every impact of sound, color, odor grew even more bitter. Those people annoyed me. I had been born in a not dissimilar environment, my uncles, my

cousins, my father were like that, of a domineering cor-
diality. They were ceremonious, usually very sociable;
every question sounded on their lips like an order barely
disguised by a false good humor, and if necessary they
could be vulgarly insulting and violent. My mother was
ashamed of the rude nature of my father and his relatives,
she wanted to be different; within that world, she played
at being the well-dressed, well-behaved lady, but at the
first sign of conflict the mask cracked, and she, too, clung
to the actions, the language of the others, with a violence
that was no different. I observed her, amazed and disappointed, and determined not to be like her, to become
truly different and so show her that it was useless and cruel
to frighten us with her repeated "You will never ever ever
see me again"; instead she should have changed for real, or
left home for real, left us, disappeared. How I suffered for
her and for myself, how ashamed I was to have come out
of the belly of such an unhappy person. That thought,
now, amid the confusion on the beach, made me more
anxious and my disdain for the habits of those people
grew, along with a thread of anguish.

Meanwhile the moving process had hit a snag. There
was a small family to whom the pregnant woman couldn't
manage to explain herself, another language, foreigners,
they wanted to stay under their umbrella. The children
tried to convince them, the dark cousins, the fierce old
man: nothing. Then I realized that they were talking to
Gino, they were looking in my direction. He and the pregnant woman came toward me like a delegation.

The young man, embarrassed, pointed out to me the
foreigners—father, mother, two small boys. Germans, he
called them, and asked if I knew the language, if I would

act as interpreter, and the woman, holding one hand behind her back and thrusting her naked belly forward, added in dialect that with those people you couldn't understand anything, I was to tell them that it was just a matter of changing umbrellas, no more, to enable the Neapolitans to stay together, friends and relatives, they were having a party.

I gave Gino a cold nod of assent and went to talk to the Germans, who turned out to be Dutch. I felt Nina's eyes on me, and spoke in a loud, confident voice. With my first words, I felt, I don't know why, a desire to show off my skills, and I conversed with enthusiasm. The head of the family was persuaded, the air of friendliness returned, Dutch and Neapolitans mingled. When I returned to my umbrella, I walked by Nina on purpose and for the first time saw her from close up. She seemed to me less beautiful, not as young, the waxing at her groin had been done badly, the child she held in her arms had a red runny eye, a forehead pimpled with sweat, and the doll was ugly and dirty. I returned to my place, outwardly calm but in fact extremely agitated.

I tried again to read, without success. I thought not of what I had said to the Dutch people but of the tone I had used. I had the suspicion that without wanting to I had been the messenger of that overbearing disorder, that I had translated into another language what was in substance a discourtesy. I was angry now, with the Neapolitans, with myself. So, when the pregnant woman pointed to me with a grimace of impatience and turned to the children, to the men, to Gino, and cried, this lady also has to move—right, signora, you'll move?, I answered brusquely, with hostile severity: no, I'm fine here, I'm sorry but I have no desire to move.

7

I left at sunset as usual, but tense and resentful. After my refusal the pregnant woman had grown insistent, in an increasingly aggressive tone, and the old man had come over and said things like what's it to you, you do us a favor today we do one for you tomorrow; but it all lasted just a few minutes, maybe I didn't even have time to say no again, clearly, but confined myself to shaking my head. The matter was ended by an abrupt remark from Nina's husband, words uttered at a distance but in a loud voice: that's enough, he said, we're fine like this, leave the lady alone. And they all withdrew, the young attendant last, murmuring an apology as he returned to his post.

As long as I stayed on the beach I pretended to read. In reality, all I could hear, as if amplified, was the clan's dialect, their shouts and laughter, and it kept me from concentrating. They were celebrating something, eating, drinking, singing, they seemed to think they were the only people on the beach, or anyway that our task was simply to delight in their happiness. From the supplies that had been brought on the motorboat all sorts of things emerged, a sumptuous meal, lasting for hours, with wine, desserts, liqueurs. No one glanced in my direction, no one said even a vaguely ironic word that concerned me. Only when I got dressed, and was preparing to leave, did the woman with the big belly leave the group and come toward me. She offered me a little plate with a slice of a raspberry-colored ice.

"It's my birthday," she said seriously.

I took the ice even though I didn't feel like it.

"Happy birthday. How old are you?"

"Forty-two."

I looked at the stomach, the protruding navel like an eye.

"You have a nice big belly."

She had a very satisfied expression.

"It's a girl. I never had children, and now look here."

"How much longer?"

"Two months. My sister-in-law had hers right away, I had to wait eight years."

"These things happen when they're supposed to happen. Thank you, and have a happy birthday."

I held out the plate to her after two bites, but she paid no attention.

"Do you have any children?"

"Two girls."

"Did you have them right away?"

"When I had the first I was twenty-three."

"They're grown."

"One is twenty-four, the other twenty-two."

"You seem younger. My sister-in-law says you couldn't be more than forty."

"I'm almost forty-eight."

"Lucky you, to have stayed so attractive. What's your name?"

"Leda."

"Neda?"

"Leda."

"Mine is Rosaria."

I held out the plate more decisively, and she took it.

"I was a bit anxious, earlier," I said, apologizing reluctantly.

"Sometimes the sea isn't good for us. Or is it the girls who are worrying you?"

"Children are always cause for worry."

We said goodbye; I realized that Nina was looking at us. I went through the pinewood discontentedly, now feeling in the wrong. What would it have cost me to change umbrellas, the others had done it, even the Dutch, why hadn't I? Sense of superiority, presumption. Defense of my leisure for thinking, snobbish tendency to give lessons in civility. All nonsense. I had paid so much attention to Nina only because I felt her to be physically closer, while I had given not a single glance to Rosaria, who was ugly and without pretensions. How many times they must have called her by name and I hadn't noticed. I had kept her outside my range, without curiosity, anonymous image of a woman who carries her pregnancy crudely. That's what I was, superficial. And then that remark: children are always cause for worry. Said to a woman about to bring one into the world: how stupid. Always words of contempt, skeptical or ironic. Bianca had cried to me once between her tears: you always think you're best. And Marta: why did you have us if all you do is complain about us? Fragments of words, mere syllables. The moment arrives when your children say to you with unhappy rage, why did you give me life: I walked absorbed in thought. The pine trees had a violet tinge; there was a wind. I heard a creaking noise behind me, perhaps footsteps, I turned, silence.

I began walking again. A violent blow struck my back, as if I had been hit with a billiard ball. I cried out in pain and surprise together, turned, breathless, and saw a pinecone tumbling into the undergrowth, big as a fist, closed. Now my heart was racing, and I rubbed my back hard, to get rid of the pain. Unable to recover my breath,

I looked around at the bushes, at the pines above me, tossing in the wind.

8

Once I was home, I undressed and examined myself in the mirror. Between my shoulder blades was a livid spot that looked like a mouth, dark at the edges, reddish at the center. I tried to reach it with my fingers; it hurt. When I examined my shirt, I found sticky traces of resin.

To calm myself I decided to go into the town, take a walk, have dinner out. Where had the blow come from. I searched my memory, but to no purpose. I couldn't decide if the pinecone had been thrown deliberately from the bushes or had fallen from a tree. A sudden blow, in the end, is only wonder and pain. When I pictured the sky and the pines, the pinecone fell from on high; when I thought of the undergrowth, the bushes, I saw a horizontal line traced by a projectile, the pinecone cutting through the air to land on my back.

The streets were filled with the Saturday evening crowd, all sunburned: entire families, women pushing strollers, irritated or angry fathers, young couples entwined or old ones holding hands. The smell of suntan lotion mixed with the aroma of cotton candy, of toasted almonds. The pain, like a burning ember stuck between my shoulder blades, kept me from thinking of anything except what had happened.

I felt the need to call my daughters, tell them about the accident. Marta answered, and started talking about how she was doing, non-stop and shrill. I had the impression that she was more than usually afraid I might interrupt, with some insidious question, a reproof, or simply that I might turn her exaggerated-light-ironic tone into something serious that would have imposed on her real questions and real answers. She went on at length about a party that she and her sister had to go to, I didn't understand clearly when, if it was that evening or the following day. It meant a lot to their father, his friends would be there, not only colleagues from the university but people who worked in television, important people he wanted to impress, to show that although he was not yet fifty he had two grown daughters, well behaved, pretty. She talked and talked, and at a certain point she began complaining about the climate. Canada, she exclaimed, is an uninhabitable country, both winter and summer. She didn't even ask me how I was, or maybe she asked but gave me no space to respond. Probably also because she never mentioned her father, I heard him between one word and the next. In conversations with my daughters I hear omitted words or phrases. Sometimes they get mad, they say Mama, I never said that, you're saying it, you invented it. But I invent nothing; you just have to listen—the unspoken says more than the spoken. That night, while Marta rambled on with her torrents of words, I imagined for an instant that she was not yet born, that she had never come out of my womb but was in someone else's—Rosaria's, for example—and would be born with a different look, a different reactivity. Maybe that was what she had always secretly desired, not to be my daughter. She was telling me about herself neurotically, from a distant continent. She was talking about her hair, about how she had to wash it constantly because it never came out right, about the hairdresser who had ruined it, and so she wasn't going to the party, she would never go out of the house with her hair looking like that, Bianca would go alone, because her hair was beautiful, and she spoke as if it were my fault, I hadn't made her in such a way that she could be happy. Old reproaches. I felt that she was frivolous, yes, frivolous and boring, situated in a space too far away from this other space, at the sea, in the evening, and I lost her. While she went on complaining, my eyes focused on the pain in my back and I saw Rosaria, fat, tired, following me through the pinewood with the gang of boys, her relatives, and she squatted, her big bare belly resting like a cupola on her broad thighs, and pointed to me as the target. When I hung up, I was sorry I had called, I felt more agitated than before; my heart was pounding.

I had to eat, but the restaurants were too crowded; I hate being a woman alone in a restaurant on a Saturday. I decided to get something in the bar near the house. I arrived wearily, and looked in the glass case beneath the counter: swarm of flies. I got two potato croquettes, an orange, a beer. I ate without much enthusiasm, listening to a group of old men behind me chattering in a thick dialect. They were playing cards, raucously; coming in I had just glimpsed them out of the corner of my eye. I turned. At the card players' table was Giovanni, the caretaker who had welcomed me on my arrival, and whom I hadn't seen since.

He left his cards on the table, joined me at the counter. He made vague conversation, how was I, had I settled in, how was the apartment, chitchat. But the whole time he was smiling at me in a complicitous manner, even though there was no reason to smile like that; we had met once, for a few minutes, and I couldn't understand what there was that we could be complicitous in. He kept his voice very low, and with every word advanced a few inches closer; twice he touched my arm with his fingertip, once he laid a hand covered with dark spots on my shoulder. When he asked if he could do anything for me he was practically whispering in my ear. I observed that his companions were staring at us silently, and I felt embarrassed. They were his age, around seventy, and, like an audience at the theatre, appeared to be watching, incredulous, an astonishing scene. When I finished eating, Giovanni nodded to the man behind the counter, in a way that meant it's on me, and there was no way I could manage to pay. I thanked him and left in a hurry; only when I crossed the threshold and heard the loud laughter of the players did I realize that that man must have boasted of some intimacy with me, the stranger, and that he had tried to prove it by assuming for the onlookers attitudes of a lord and master.

I should have been angry, but I felt abruptly better. I thought of going back into the bar, sitting down beside Giovanni, and visibly rooting for him in the card game, like a blond bimbo in a gangster movie. What was he, in the end: a lean old man, with all his hair, only the skin spotted and deeply lined, the irises yellow and the pupils faintly veiled. I would have whispered in his ear, rubbed my breast against his arm, put my chin on his shoulder as I peered at his cards. He would have been grateful to me for the rest of his days.

Instead I went home and waited on the terrace for sleep to come, while the beam of the lighthouse struck.

9

I didn't close my eyes all night. My back was inflamed and throbbing, and from all over town came loud music, car noises, cries of greeting and farewell, right up until dawn.

I lay on the bed but restlessly, with a growing sensation of flaking layers: Bianca and Marta, the difficulties in my work, Nina, Elena, Rosaria, my parents, Nina's husband, the books I was reading, Gianni, my ex-husband. At dawn there was a sudden silence and I slept for several hours.

I woke at eleven, gathered up my things quickly, and got in the car. But it was Sunday, a very hot Sunday: I ran into a lot of traffic, had trouble parking, and ended up in a chaos greater than that of the day before, a stream of young people, old people, children, loaded down with gear, jamming the path through the pinewood and pressing forward to lay claim as soon as possible to a slice of sand and sea.

Gino, occupied by the continuous flow of bathers, paid little attention to me, only giving a nod of greeting. Once in my bathing suit, I lay down quickly in the shade, face up to hide the bruise on my back, and put on my dark glasses; my head ached.

The beach was packed. I looked around for Rosaria, and didn't see her; the clan seemed to have dispersed, mingling with the crowd. Only by looking carefully could I pick out Nina and her husband walking along the shore.

She was wearing a blue two-piece suit, and again seemed to me very beautiful, moving with her usual natural elegance, even if at that moment she was speaking heatedly. He, without a T-shirt, was stockier than his sister Rosaria, pale, without even a touch of red from the sun; his movements were measured, on his hairy chest was a cross on a gold chain, and he had—a feature that seemed repellent—a large belly, divided into two bulging halves of flesh by a deep scar that ran from the top of his bathing suit to the arc of his ribs.

I marveled at the absence of Elena, it was the first time I hadn't seen mother and daughter together. But then I realized that the child was near me, alone, sitting on the sand in the sun, her mother's new hat on her head, playing with the doll. I noticed that her eye was still red; occasionally she licked the mucus that dripped from her nose with the tip of her tongue.

Whom did she look like? Now that I had seen her father, too, it seemed to me that I could distinguish in her the features of both parents. One looks at a child and immediately the game of resemblances begins, as one hurries to enclose that child within the known perimeter of the parents. In fact it's just live matter, yet another random bit of flesh descended from long chains of organisms. Engineering—nature is engineering, so is culture, science is right behind, only chaos is not an engineer—and, along with it, the furious need to reproduce. I had wanted Bianca, one wants a child with an animal opacity reinforced by popular beliefs. She had arrived immediately, I was twenty-three, her father and I were right in the midst of a difficult struggle to keep jobs at the university. He made it, I didn't. A woman's body does a thousand different things, toils, runs, studies, fantasizes, invents, wearies, and meanwhile the breasts enlarge, the lips of the sex swell, the flesh throbs with a round life that is yours, your life, and yet pushes elsewhere, draws away from you although it inhabits your belly, joyful and weighty, felt as a greedy impulse and yet repellent, like an insect's poison injected into a vein.

Your life wants to become another's. Bianca was expelled, expelled herself, but—everyone around us believed it, and we, too, believed it—she couldn't grow up alone, how sad, she needed a brother, a sister for company. So, right after her, I planned, yes, just as they say, *planned*, Marta to grow in my belly, too.

I was twenty-five and every other game was over for me. Their father was racing around the world, one opportunity after another. He didn't even have time to look carefully at what had been copied from his body, at how the reproduction had turned out. He barely glanced at the two little girls, but he said, with real tenderness: they are identical to you. Gianni is a kind man, our daughters love him. He took little or no care of them, but when it was necessary he did everything he could, even now he is doing everything he can. Children generally like him. If he were here, he wouldn't stay, like me, on the lounge chair but would go and play with Elena: he would feel it his duty to do so.

Me no. I watched the child, but, seeing her like that, alone and yet with all her ancestors compressed into her flesh, I felt something like repugnance, even though I didn't know what repelled me. The little girl was playing with the doll. She spoke to it, but not as to a mangy-looking doll, with a half blond, half bald head. Who knows what character she imagined for her. Nani, she said, Nanuccia, Nanicchia, Nennella. It was an affectionate game. She kissed her hard on the face, so hard that the plastic almost seemed to inflate as her mouth exhaled her gassy, vibrant love, all the loving she was capable of. She kissed her on her bare breast, on her back, on her stomach, everywhere, with her mouth open as if to eat her.

I turned away, one shouldn't watch children's games. But then I looked at her again. Nani was an ugly old doll, her face and body showed marks from a ballpoint pen. Yet in those moments a living force was released. Now it was she who kissed Elena with increasing frenzy. She kissed her lips with determination, she kissed her slender chest, her slightly swelling stomach, she pressed her head against the green bathing suit. The child realized that I was looking at her. She smiled at me with an abrasive gaze and as if in defiance hugged the doll's head between her legs, with both hands. Children play games like this, of course, then they forget. I got up. The sun was burning, I was very sweaty. There wasn't a breath of wind, on the horizon a gray mist was rising. I went to swim.

From the water, floating lazily in the Sunday crowd, I saw Nina and her husband continuing to argue. She was protesting, he was listening. Then the man seemed tired of talking, he said something decisive to her but without getting upset, calmly. He must truly love her, I thought. He left her on the shore and went to confer with those who had arrived the day before in the motorboat. Evidently they were the object of contention. It always happened like that, I knew from experience: first the party, friends, relatives, everyone loves each other; then the quarrels of close quarters, old resentments that explode. Nina couldn't tolerate the guests any longer and, look, her husband was sending them away. After a while the men, the women of ostentatious wealth, the obese children abandoned, in no particular order, the clan's umbrellas; they loaded their things onto the motorboat, and Nina's husband helped them himself, perhaps to hurry their departure. They left as they had arrived, amid hugs and kisses, but none of them said goodbye to Nina. She for her part went off along the beach with her head down, as if she couldn't bear to look at them a moment longer.

I swam a good distance, in order to leave behind the crowd. The sea water soothed my back, the pain ceased, or it seemed to me that it ceased. I stayed in the water a long time, until I saw that my fingertips were wrinkled and I began to tremble with cold. My mother, when she realized I was in that state, would drag me out of the water, yelling. When she saw that my teeth were chattering she became even more furious, yanked me, covered me from head to toe with a towel, rubbed me with such an energy, such violence that I didn't know if it was really worry for my health or a long-fostered rage, a ferocity, that chafed my skin.

I spread the towel directly on the burning sand and lay down. How I love the hot sand after the sea has chilled my body. I looked where Elena had been. Only the doll remained, but in a painful position, arms spread, legs apart, lying on her back, her head half buried in the sand. Her nose could be seen, an eye, half her skull. I fell asleep because of the heat, the sleepless night.

10

I slept a minute, ten. When I woke, I stood up dazed. I saw that the sky had turned white, a hot white lead. The air was still, the crowd had grown, there was a clamor of music and human beings. In that Sunday throng, as if by a sort of secret call, the first person who leaped to my eyes was Nina.

Something was happening to her. She was moving slowly among the umbrellas, hesitant, her mouth working. She
turned her head to one side, to the other, as if mechanically, like a bird in alarm. She said something to herself, from
where I was I couldn't tell what, then she hurried toward
her husband, who was on a chair under the umbrella.

The man jumped to his feet, looked around. The severe
old man pulled him by an arm, he wriggled free, went over
to Rosaria. All the family, big and small, began to look
around as if they were a single body, then they moved,
scattered.

Calls began: Elena, Lenuccia, Lena. Rosaria walked
with short but quick steps toward the sea as if she had an
urgent need to go in. I looked at Nina. She made senseless
gestures, she touched her forehead, she went to the right,
then turned abruptly back to the left. It was as if from her
very guts something were sucking the life from her face.
Her skin turned yellow, her lively eyes were mad with anxiety. She couldn't find the child, she had lost her.

She'll turn up, I thought: I had experience with getting
lost. My mother said that as a child all I did was get lost.
In an instant I would vanish, she would have to run to the
bath house and ask them to announce on the loudspeaker
what I looked like, that I was called such and such, and
meanwhile she would stay at the counter and wait. I did-
n't remember anything about my vanishing, my memory
held other things. I was afraid that it was my mother who
would get lost, I lived in the anxiety of not being able to
find her. But I remembered clearly when I had lost Bianca.
I was running along the beach like Nina now, but I had
Marta bawling in my arms. I didn't know what to do, I was
alone with the two children, my husband was abroad, I

knew no one. A child, yes, is a vortex of anxieties. It remained impressed on me that I had looked in every direction except toward the sea: I didn't dare even to glance at the water.

I realized that Nina was doing the same thing. She was searching everywhere but she desperately kept her back to the sea, and suddenly I was moved, I felt like crying. From that moment I could no longer stand aside; I found it intolerable that the crowd on the beach didn't even notice the frantic searching of the Neapolitans. There are movements so rapid that no draftsman can reproduce them, one is luminous, the other dark. Those who had appeared so autonomous, so overweening, seemed to me fragile. I admired Rosaria, who alone was searching the sea. With her large belly she walked, with her, but short steps, along the shore. I got up then, joined Nina, touched her arm. She turned suddenly, with a snakelike motion, and cried you've found her, speaking to me as if we knew each other well, even though we had never exchanged a word.

"She's wearing your hat," I told her, "she'll be found, we'll see her easily."

She looked at me uncertainly, then nodded yes, ran in the direction in which her husband had vanished. She ran like a young athlete in a contest with a good or bad fate.

I set off in the opposite direction, along the first row of umbrellas, slowly. It seemed to me that I was Elena, or Bianca when she was lost, but perhaps I was only myself as a child, climbing back out of oblivion. A child who gets lost on the beach sees everything unchanged and yet no longer recognizes anything. She is without orientation, something that before had made bathers and umbrellas recognizable. The child feels that she is exactly where she was and yet doesn't know where she is. She looks around with frightened eyes and sees that the sea is the sea, the beach is the beach, the people are the people, the fresh-coconut seller is really the fresh-coconut seller. Yet every thing or person is alien to her and so she cries. To the unknown adult who asks her what's wrong, why is she crying, she doesn't say that she's lost, she says that she can't find her mama. Bianca was crying when they found her, when they brought her back to me. I was crying, too, with happiness, with relief, but meanwhile I was also screaming with rage, like my mother, because of the crushing weight of responsibility, the bond that strangles, and with my free arm I dragged my firstborn, yelling, you'll pay for this, Bianca, you'll see when we get home, you must never go off again—never.

I walked for a while looking among the children, by themselves, in groups, in the arms of adults. I was in a turmoil, slightly sick to my stomach, but I was able to pay attention. Finally I saw the straw hat, and my heart skipped a beat. From a distance it seemed abandoned on the sand, but underneath it was Elena. She was sitting a few feet from the water, people passed her by without paying any attention; she was crying, a slow flow of silent tears. She didn't say that she had lost her mother, she said that she had lost her doll. She was desperate.

I picked her up in my arms and returned quickly toward the bath house. I met Rosaria, who almost tore her away from me with an enthusiastic fury, she shouted with joy, waved at her sister-in-law. Nina saw us, saw her daughter, ran. Her husband, too, ran, all of them, from the dunes, from the bath house, from the shore. All the members of the family wanted to kiss, hug, touch Elena, even though she continued to weep, and to taste some satisfaction of her own for the danger escaped.

I withdrew, returned to the umbrella, began to gather up my things, even though it wasn't even two in the afternoon. I didn't like it that Elena was still crying. I saw that the group was celebrating her, the women took her from her mother and passed her around to try to quiet her, but without success, the child was inconsolable.

Nina came over to me. Immediately afterward Rosaria also arrived, she seemed proud of having been the first to establish a relationship with me, who had been so decisive.

"I wanted to thank you," said Nina.

"It was a good scare."

"I thought I would die."

"My daughter got lost on a Sunday in August, almost twenty years ago, but I couldn't see anything—anguish is blinding. In this situation strangers are more useful."

"Luckily you were there," Rosaria said. "So many bad things happen." Then evidently her gaze fell on my back, because she exclaimed with a gesture of horror, "My goodness, what happened here, to your back, what was it?"

"A pinecone, in the woods."

"It looks painful—did you put something on it?"

She wanted to go and get an ointment she had, she said it was miraculous. Nina and I remained alone; the cries of the child reached us insistently.

"She won't calm down," I said.

Nina smiled.

"It's a bad day: we found her and she lost her doll."

"You'll find it."

"Of course, if we don't find her, what will we do—she'll get sick."

I felt a sudden sensation of cold on my back, Rosaria had come up behind me silently and was spreading her cream.

"How is it?"

"Good, thank you."

She continued, attentively. When she had finished, I put my dress on over my bathing suit, picked up my bag.

"Until tomorrow," I said. I was in a hurry to get away.

"You'll see, already by tonight it'll feel better."

"Yes."

I looked again at Elena, who was wriggling and writhing in her father's arms, calling alternately for her mother and the doll.

"Let's go," Rosaria said to her sister-in-law, "let's find the doll, because I can't stand hearing her scream anymore."

Nina gave me a nod of farewell, went off to her daughter. Rosaria instead began immediately to ask children and parents, searching meanwhile, without permission, among the toys piled under the umbrellas.

I went back up over the dunes, and into the pinewood, but even there I seemed to hear the child's cries. I was confused, placed a hand on my chest to calm my racing heart. I had taken the doll, she was in my bag.

11

As I drove home I grew calmer. I discovered that I couldn't recall the exact moment of an action that I now considered almost comic, comic because senseless. I felt like someone at the moment of realizing, perhaps with fear, perhaps with amusement: look what happened to me.

I must have had one of those waves of compassion that, from the time I was a child, have engulfed me, with no obvious reason, for people, animals, plants, things. I liked the explanation; it seemed to allude to something intrinsically noble. It had been a spontaneous impulse to help, I thought. Nena, Nani, Nennella, or whatever her name was. I saw her abandoned in the sand, limbs askew, her face half buried, as if she were about to suffocate, and I picked her up. An infantile reaction, nothing special, we never really grow up. I decided that I would give her back the next day. I'll go to the beach very early, I'll stick her in the sand just where Elena left her, I'll do it in such a way that she'll find the doll herself. I'll play with the child a little and then say, look, she's here, let's dig. I felt almost happy.

At home I took bathing suits and towels and lotions out of my bag, but I left the doll in the bottom, to be sure, the next day, not to forget her. I took a shower, washed my bathing suits, hung them out to dry. I also made a salad and ate it on the terrace, looking at the sea, at the foam around the tongues of lava, at the array of black clouds leaving the horizon. Then suddenly it seemed to me I had done something mean, unintentional but mean. A gesture like one you make in sleep, when you turn over in bed and upset the lamp on the night table. Compassion doesn't have anything to do with it, I thought, there was no question of a generous feeling. I felt like a drop that slides over a leaf after the rain, carried along by a clearly inevitable movement. Now I'm trying to find excuses, but there are none. I feel confused, the months of lightness are already gone, perhaps; I'm afraid that racing thoughts and whirling images are returning. The sea is becoming a violet band, the wind has come up. How changeable the weather is, the temperature has fallen abruptly. On the beach Elena must still be crying, Nina is desperate, Rosaria has combed the sand, inch by inch, the clan must be at war with all the other beachgoers by now. A paper napkin flew away, I cleared the table; and for the first time in many months I felt alone. I saw in the distance, on the sea, curtains of dark rain falling from the clouds.

In the space of a few minutes the wind had gained strength, moaning as it whipped against the building and blowing dust, dry leaves, dead insects into the house. I closed the door to the terrace, took the bag, sat down on the small sofa in front of the window. I couldn't even hold on to my intentions. I fished out the doll, turned her in bewilderment between my hands. No clothes, who knows where Elena had left them. She was heavier than I expected, she must be full of water. Her sparse blond hair stuck out of her head in widely scattered tufts. Her cheeks were too puffy, she had stupid blue eyes and small lips with a dark opening at the center. Her chest was long, her stomach protruding; between short fat legs one could just make out a vertical line that continued without a break between broad buttocks.

I would have liked to dress her. I had the idea of buying her some clothes as a surprise for Elena, a kind of reparation. What is a doll to a child. I had had one with beautiful curly hair, I had taken great care of her, had never lost her. Her name was Mina, my mother said that I had given her the name. Mina, mammina. *Mammuccia* came to mind, a word for "doll" that hasn't been used for a long time. Play with the *mammuccia*. My mother had rarely yielded to the games I tried to play with her body. She immediately got nervous, she didn't like being the doll. She laughed, pulled away, grew angry. It annoyed her when I combed her hair, put ribbons in it, washed her face and ears, undressed her, redressed her.

I, on the other hand, no. As an adult I tried to keep in mind the misery of not being able to handle the hair, the face, the body of my mother. So when Bianca was a small child I patiently became her doll. She dragged me under the kitchen table, it was our playhouse, and made me lie down. I was very tired, I remember: Marta wouldn't sleep at night, only during the day, and then only a little, and Bianca was always around me, full of demands, she didn't want to go to day care; when I did manage to leave her there she got sick, complicating my existence even further. Yet I tried to keep my nerves under control, I wanted to be a good mother. I lay on the floor, let myself be cared for as if I were sick. Bianca gave me medicine, brushed my teeth, combed my hair. Sometimes I fell asleep, but she was little and didn't know how to use the comb, and when she pulled my hair I started, and woke. I felt my eyes tearing with pain.

I was so desolate in those years. I could no longer study, I played without joy, my body felt inanimate, without desires. When Marta began to howl in the other room it was almost a liberation. I got up, rudely cutting off Bianca's game, but I felt innocent, it wasn't I who was leaving my daughter, it was my second-born who was tearing me away from the first. I have to go to Marta, I'll be right back, wait. She would begin crying.

It was in a moment of feeling generally inadequate that I decided to give Mina to Bianca; it seemed to me a fine gesture, a way of relieving her envy for her little sister. So

I fished the old doll out of a cardboard box on top of the wardrobe and said to Bianca: see, her name is Mina, this was Mama's doll when she was little, I'm giving her to you. I thought she would love her; I was sure she would devote herself to her as she had devoted herself to me in our games. Instead she put her aside, she didn't like Mina. She preferred an ugly rag doll with stringy yellow yarn hair her father had brought as a present from somewhere or other. I was hurt.

One day Bianca happened to be playing on the balcony: it was a place she really liked. As soon as spring arrived I would leave her there; I didn't have time to take her outside, but I wanted her to have air and sun, even if the noise of the traffic and a strong smell of exhaust rose from the street. I hadn't been able to open a book for months; I was exhausted and angry; there was never enough money, I barely slept. I found Bianca sitting on Mina, as if she were a chair, and meanwhile playing with her doll. I told her to get up right away, she mustn't ruin something that was dear to me from my childhood: she was really cruel and ungrateful. I called her ungrateful, and I yelled, I think I yelled that giving her the doll had been a mistake, she was my doll and I would take her back.

How many things are done and said to children behind the closed doors of houses. Bianca was already a cool character, she's always been like that, swallowing up anxieties and feelings. She remained sitting on Mina; measuring her words, the way she still does when she declares her wishes, as if they were her last: no, it's mine. Then I gave her a nasty shove: she was a child of three but at that moment she seemed older, stronger than me. I tore Mina away from her and finally her eyes showed fear. I discovered that she had taken off the doll's clothes, even her little shoes and socks, and had scribbled all over her, from head to foot, with markers. It was a disfigurement that could be corrected but to me it seemed without remedy. Everything in those years seemed to me without remedy, I myself was without remedy. I hurled the doll over the railing of the balcony.

I saw her fly toward the asphalt and felt a cruel joy. She seemed to me, as she fell, an ugly creature. I stood leaning against the railing for I don't know how long watching the cars that passed over her, mutilating her. Then I realized that Bianca, too, was watching, on her knees, with her forehead pressed against the bars of the railing. I picked her up, she let herself be held, yielding. I kissed her for a long time, I hugged her as if I wanted to take her back into my body. You hurt me, Mama, you're hurting me. I left Elena's doll on the sofa, lying on her back, belly up.

The storm had moved quickly to land, violently, with blinding lightning and thunder that sounded like cars exploding, full of dynamite. I ran to close the windows in the bedroom before everything got soaked, I turned on the bedside lamp. I lay on the bed, arranged the pillows against the headboard, and began to work with a will, filling pages with notes.

Reading, writing have always been my way of soothing myself.

12

A reddish light roused me from my work: it was no longer raining. I spent some time putting on makeup, dressing with care. I wanted to look like a respectable lady, perfectly proper. I went out.

The Sunday evening crowd was less dense and noisy than Saturday's, the extraordinary weekend flood was diminishing. I walked along the sea a little, then headed toward a restaurant next to the market. I ran into Gino: he was dressed the way he always was at the beach, maybe he was just returning. He nodded respectfully in greeting, and wished to pass on, but I stopped and so he was compelled to stop as well.

I felt the need to hear the sound of my voice, to get it under control with the help of someone else's voice. I asked him about the storm, what had happened on the beach. He said there had been a strong wind, a tempest of water and wind, many of the umbrellas had been overturned. People had run for shelter to the bath house, the bar, but the crush had been too great and most had given up, the beach emptied.

"Luckily you left early."

"I like storms."

"Your books and notebooks would get ruined."

"Did your book get wet?"

"A little."

"What are you studying?"

"Law."

"How much longer do you have?"

"I'm behind, I've wasted time. Do you teach at the university?"

"Yes."

"What?"

"English literature."

"I saw that you know a lot of languages."

I laughed.

"I don't know anything really well, I also wasted some time. I work twelve hours a day at the university and I'm everyone's slave."

We walked a little, I relaxed. I talked about this and that to put him at his ease, and meanwhile I saw myself from the outside: I dressed like a proper lady, he covered with sand, in shorts, T-shirt, flip-flops. I was amused, even rather pleased; if Bianca and Marta had seen me I would have been teased no end.

He was certainly their age: a male child, a slender nervous body to care for. The young male bodies that had attracted me as an adolescent were like that, tall, thin, very dark, like Marta's boyfriends, not small, fair, a little stocky and plump, like Bianca's young men, always a little older than she, with veins as blue as their eyes. But I loved them all, my daughters' first boyfriends, I bestowed on them an exaggerated affection. I wanted to reward them, perhaps, because they had recognized the beauty, the good qualities of my daughters, and so had freed them from the anguish of being ugly, the certainty of having no power of seduction. Or I wanted to reward them because they had providentially saved me, too, from bad moods and conflicts and complaints and attempts to soothe my daughters: I'm ugly, I'm fat; but I, too, felt ugly and fat at your age; no, you weren't ugly and fat, you were beautiful; you, too, are beautiful, you don't even realize how people look at you; they're not looking at us, they're looking at you.

At whom were the looks of desire directed. When Bianca was fifteen and Marta thirteen, I was not yet forty. Their childs' bodies softened almost together. For a while

I continued to think that the gazes of men on the street were directed at me, as had happened for twenty-five years; it had become habitual to receive them, to endure them. Then I realized that they slid lewdly from me to rest on the girls; I was alarmed, and gratified. Finally I said to myself with ironic wistfulness: a stage is about to end.

Yet I began to pay more attention to myself, as if I wanted to keep the body I was accustomed to, put off its departure. When my daughters' boyfriends came to the house, I tried to make myself more attractive to receive them. I barely saw them, when they entered, when they left, saying goodbye to me in embarrassment, and yet I was very careful about my appearance, my manners. Bianca took them into her room, Marta into hers, I was alone. I wanted my daughters to be loved, I couldn't bear them not to be, I was terrified of their possible unhappiness; but the gusts of sensuality they exhaled were violent, voracious, and I felt that the force of attraction of their bodies was as if subtracted from mine. So I was content when they told me, laughing, that the boys had found me a young and good-looking mother. It seemed to me for a few minutes that our three organisms had reached a pleasant accord.

Once, I was perhaps excessively flirtatious with a friend of Bianca's, a surly fifteen-year-old, practically mute, with an unwashed and suffering appearance. When he left, I called my daughter, she came to my room: she and then, out of curiosity, Marta.

"Did your friend like the cake?"

"Yes."

"I should have put chocolate on it, but I didn't have a chance, maybe next time."

"Next time, he said, if you'd give him a blow job."

"Bianca, what kind of language is that?"

"That's what he said."

"He didn't."

"He did."

Gradually I yielded. I taught myself to be present only if they wanted me present and to speak only if they asked me to speak. It was what they required of me and I gave it to them. What I wanted of them I never understood, I don't know even now.

I looked at Gino, I thought: I'll ask him if he'll have dinner with me. I also thought: He'll invent an excuse, he'll say no, never mind. Instead he said only, but timidly:

"I should go and take a shower, change."

"You're fine like that."

"I don't even have my wallet."

"I'm inviting you."

Gino made an effort at conversation during the entire meal—even attempting to make me laugh—but we had almost nothing in common. He knew that he had to entertain me between one mouthful and the next, he knew that he had to avoid silences that were too long, and he did his best, he hurled himself onto the most diverse paths, like a lost animal.

Of himself he had little to say, he tried to make me talk about myself. But his questions were stiff, and I read in his eyes that he had no real interest in my answers. Although I tried to help him, I couldn't escape the fact that the topics of conversation were quickly being used up.

First he asked about what I was studying, I told him I was preparing a course for the next year.

"On what."

"*Olivia.*"

"What's that?"

"A story."

"Is it long?"

He liked short exams, he was very annoyed by professors who pile on the books to show that their exam is important. He had big white teeth, a wide mouth. His eyes were small, almost slits. He gesticulated a lot, he laughed. He knew nothing of *Olivia*, nothing of what I was passionate about. Like my daughters, who, growing up, had stayed cautiously away from my interests, had studied science, physics, like their father.

I spoke a little about them, saying a lot of nice things but in an ironic tone. At last, slowly, we fell back on what we did have in common: the beach, the bath house, his employer, the people on the beach. He talked to me about the foreigners, almost always pleasant, and the Italians, pretentious and arrogant. He spoke with sympathy of the Africans, of the Asian girls who went from umbrella to umbrella. But only when he began to speak of Nina and her family did I understand that I was there, in that restaurant with him, for this.

He told me about the doll, about the child's desperation.

"After the storm I looked everywhere, I raked the sand until an hour ago, but I couldn't find it."

"It will turn up."

"I hope so, especially for the mother: they're furious with her, as if it were her fault."

He alluded to Nina with admiration.

"She's been coming here on vacation since her daughter was born. Her husband rents a villa in the dunes. You can't see the house from the beach. It's in the pinewood, it's a beautiful place."

He said that she was a really well brought up girl, she had finished high school and had even gone, briefly, to the university.

"She's very pretty," I said.

"Yes, she's beautiful."

They had talked a few times—I gathered—and she had told him she wanted to go back to her studies.

"She's only a year older than I am."

"Twenty-five?"

"Twenty-three, I'm twenty-two."

"Like my daughter Marta."

He was silent for a moment, then said suddenly, with a dark look that made him ugly:

"Have you seen her husband? Would you ever have made your daughter marry someone like that?"

I asked, ironically:

"What's wrong with him, what don't you like?"

He shook his head, and said seriously:

"Everything. Him, his friends and relatives. His sister is unbearable."

"Rosaria, the pregnant lady?"

"Lady, her? Forget about her, it's better. I admired you yesterday, when you wouldn't move from your umbrella. But don't do things like that anymore."

"Why?"

The boy shrugged his shoulders, shook his head unhappily.

"They're bad people."

13

I got home around midnight. We had finally found a

subject that interested both of us and the time passed quickly. I learned from Gino that the fat gray-haired woman was Nina's mother. I learned also that the stern old man was named Corrado and wasn't her father but Rosaria's husband. It was like discussing a film that one has watched without fully understanding the relationship between the characters, at times not even knowing their names, and when we said good night it seemed to me that I had a clearer idea. Only about Nina's husband had I learned little or nothing, Gino said his name was Toni, he came on Saturday and left Monday morning. I understood that he hated him, he didn't even want to speak about him. And I, besides, felt very little curiosity about that man.

The boy waited politely until I had closed the street door behind me. I climbed the dimly lighted stairs to the fourth floor. Bad people, he had said. What could they do to me. I went into the apartment, turned on the light, and saw the doll supine on the sofa, her arms turned up to the ceiling, her legs spread, her face toward me. The Neapolitans had turned the beach upside down to find her, Gino had doggedly searched the sand with his rake. I wandered through the rooms, the only sound was the hum of the refrigerator in the kitchen; the town, too, seemed to be quiet. I discovered, looking at myself in the bathroom mirror, that my face was drawn, my eyes puffy. I chose a clean T-shirt and got ready for bed, although I wasn't sleepy.

The evening with Gino had been pleasant, but I felt that something had left me with a vague irritation. I opened the door onto the terrace, a fresh breeze came from the sea, the sky was without stars. He likes Nina, I thought, it doesn't take much to see that. And, instead of being touched or amused, I felt a pang of discontent that reached toward the girl, as if, appearing every day on the beach and attracting him, she had taken something away from me.

I moved the doll, lay down on the sofa. If Gino had met Bianca and Marta, I wondered almost out of habit, which of the two would he have liked more. Since my daughters' early adolescence, I had had this passion for comparing them with their friends, close friends, classmates who were considered pretty, who were successful. In a confused way I felt that they were rivals of the two girls, as if the others' exceptional self-confidence, seductiveness, grace, intelligence took something away from my daughters and, in some obscure way, from me. I controlled myself, I spoke kindly, yet I tended to demonstrate silently to myself that they were all less pretty or, if pretty, unlikable, empty, and I would list the quirks, the stupidities, the temporary defects of those growing bodies. Sometimes, when I saw Bianca or Marta suffer because they felt outdone, I couldn't resist, I intervened rudely with their friends who were too extroverted, too attractive, too ingratiating.

When Marta was around fourteen she had had a class mate named Florinda. Florinda, although she was the same age, was not a girl—she was already a woman, and very beautiful. With every gesture, every smile I saw how she overshadowed my daughter and I suffered to think that they went to school together, to parties, on outings; it seemed to me that as long as my daughter remained in that company life would continue to escape her.

On the other hand Marta was very attached to her friendship with Florinda—was violently taken with her— and it seemed to me a difficult and risky enterprise to separate them. For a while I tried to console her for that permanent humiliation by sticking to generalities, without ever using Florinda's name. I kept telling her: how pretty you are, Marta, how sweet, you have such intelligent eyes, you look just like your grandmother and she was a real beauty. Vain words. She thought she was not only less attractive than her friend but less attractive than her sister, than everyone, and listening to me she became more depressed, she said I was saying those things because I was her mother, and sometimes she murmured: I won't listen to you, Mama, you don't see me for what I am, leave me alone, mind your own business.

At that time I had a constant stomachache from tension, from a sense of guilt: I thought that any unhappiness in my daughters was caused by a now proved failure of my love. So I soon became more insistent. I said to her: you really do look like my mother, and I brought up my own case, telling her: when I was your age, I was sure that I was ugly, I thought: my mother is pretty but I'm not. Marta let me know, multiplying her signs of annoyance, that she couldn't wait for me to stop talking.

So it happened that, in consoling her, I felt more and more disconsolate myself. I thought: who knows how beauty is reproduced. I remembered too well how, at Marta's age, I had been certain that my mother, in creating me, had separated herself from me, as when one has an impulse of revulsion and, with a gesture, pushes away the plate. I suspected that she had begun to flee the moment she had me in her womb, even though as I grew up everyone said that I resembled her. There were resemblances, but they seemed to me faded. Not even when I discovered that I was attractive to men was I appeased. She emanated a vital warmth, whereas I felt cold, as if I had veins of metal. I wanted to be like her not only in the image in the mirror or in the stasis of photographs. I wanted to be like her in the capacity she had to expand and become essence on the streets, in the subway or the funicular, in the shops, under the eyes of strangers. No instrument of reproduction can capture that enchanted aura. Not even the pregnant belly can replicate it precisely.

But Florinda had that aura. When she and Marta came home from school one rainy afternoon, and I saw them walk through the hall, the living room, in heavy shoes, carelessly spotting the floor with mud and water, and then go into the kitchen, grab some cookies, amuse themselves by breaking them into pieces and eating them as they went through the house, leaving crumbs everywhere, I felt for that splendid adolescent girl, so self-assured, an uncontainable aversion. I said to her: Florinda, who do you think you are, do you behave like that at your house? Now, my dear, I want you to sweep up and then wash the floor, and don't leave until you've finished. She thought I was joking, but I took out the broom, the bucket, the mop, and must have had a fierce expression on my face, because she murmured only: Marta made a mess, too, and Marta tried to say: it's true, Mama. But my words must have been so harsh, uttered with such an indisputable severity, that they were both immediately silent. Frightened, Florinda washed the floor with care.

My daughter watched her. Afterward she shut herself in her room and wouldn't speak to me for days. She isn't like Bianca: she's fragile, she gives in at the first change of tone, she retreats without fighting. Florinda gradually disappeared from her life; every so often I asked how is your friend, and she muttered something vague or answered with a shrug.

But my anxieties didn't disappear. I observed my daughters when they weren't paying attention, I felt for them a complicated alternation of sympathy and antipathy. Bianca, I sometimes thought, is unlikable, and I suffered for her. Then I discovered that she was much loved, she had girl and boy friends, and I felt that it was only I, her mother, who found her unlikable, and was remorseful. I didn't like her dismissive laugh. I didn't like her eagerness to always claim more than others: at the table, for example, she took more food than everyone else, not to eat it but to be sure of not missing anything, of not being neglected or cheated. I didn't like her stubborn silence when she felt she was wrong but couldn't admit her mistake.

You're like that, too, my husband told me. Maybe it was true, what seemed to me unlikable in Bianca was only the reflection of an antipathy I felt for myself. Or no, it wasn't so simple, things were more tangled. Even when I recognized in the two girls what I considered my own good qualities I felt that something wasn't right. I had the impression that they didn't know how to make good use of those qualities, that the best part of me ended up in their bodies as a mistaken graft, a parody, and I was angry, ashamed.

In fact, if I really think about it, what I loved best in my daughters was what seemed alien to me. In them—I felt— I liked most the features that came from their father, even after our marriage stormily ended. Or those which went back to ancestors of whom I knew nothing. Or those which seemed, in the combining of organisms, an ingenious invention of chance. It seemed to me, in other words, that the closer I felt to them, the less responsibility I bore for their bodies.

But that alien closeness was rare. Their troubles, their griefs, their conflicts returned to impose themselves, continuously, and I was bitter, I felt a sense of guilt. I was always, in some way, the origin of their sufferings, and the outlet. They accused me silently or yelling. They resented the unfair distribution not only of obvious resemblances but of secret ones, those we become aware of later, the aura of bodies, the aura that stuns like a strong liquor. Barely perceptible tones of voice. A small gesture, a way of batting the eyelashes, a smile-sneer. The walk, the shoulder that leans slightly to the left, a graceful swinging of the arms. The impalpable mixture of tiny movements that, combined in a certain way, make Bianca seductive, Marta not, or vice versa, and so cause pride, pain. Or hatred, because the mother's power always seems to be that she gives unfairly, beginning in the living niche of the womb.

Starting right there, according to my two girls, I had behaved cruelly. I treated one as a daughter, the other a stepdaughter. To Bianca I gave a large bosom, while Marta seems a boy; she doesn't know she's beautiful, and wears a padded bra, a ploy that humiliates her. I suffer seeing her suffer. As a young woman I had large breasts, but after her birth I didn't. You gave the best of yourself to Bianca, she repeats constantly, to me the worst. Marta is like that, she protects herself by seeing herself as deprived.

Not Bianca, no, ever since she was a child Bianca has fought me. She tried to pluck from me the secret of skills that in her eyes appeared wonderful and show that she in her turn was capable of them. It was she who revealed to me that when I peel fruit I am finicky about making sure that the knife cuts without ever breaking the peel. Before her admiration led me to discover this, I hadn't realized it, goodness knows where I learned it, maybe it's only my taste for ambitious and stubbornly precise work. Make a snake, Mama, she would say, insistent: peel the apple and make a snake, please. "*Haciendo serpentinas*," I found recently in a poem by Maria Guerra that I'm fond of. Bianca was captivated by the serpentines of the peel, they were one of the many magical abilities she attributed to me; it seems touching now when I think about it.

One morning she got a bad cut on her finger trying to show that she, too, could make a snake. She was five and was immediately in despair: the blood flowed, along with tears of disappointment. I was frightened, yelled at her: I couldn't leave her alone for a moment, there was never time for myself. I felt that I was suffocating, it seemed to me that I was betraying myself. For long minutes I refused to kiss her wound, the kiss that makes the pain go away. I wanted to teach her that you don't do that, it's dangerous, only Mama does it, who is grownup. Mama.

Poor creatures who came out of my belly, all alone now on the other side of the world. I placed the doll on my knees as if for company. Why had I taken her. She guarded the love of Nina and Elena, their bond, their reciprocal passion. She was the shining testimony of perfect motherhood. I brought her to my breast. How many damaged, lost things did I have behind me, and yet present, now, in a whirl of images. I understood clearly that I didn't want to give Nani back, even though I felt remorse, fear in keeping her with me. I kissed her face, her mouth, I hugged her as I had seen Elena do. She emitted a gurgle that seemed to me a hostile remark and, with it, a jet of brown saliva that dirtied my lips and my shirt.

14

I slept on the sofa, with the door to the terrace open, and I woke late; my head was heavy, my bones ached. It was past ten, and raining; a strong wind was agitating the sea. I looked for the doll but didn't see her. I felt anxious, as if it were possible that she had thrown herself off the terrace during the night. I looked around, hunted under the sofa, afraid that someone had come in and taken her. I found her in the kitchen, sitting on the table, in the shadows. I must have brought her in there when I went to wash my mouth and my shirt.

No beach, the weather was nasty. The plan to give Nani back to Elena today seemed to me not only weak but impractical. I went out to have breakfast, to buy the papers and something for lunch and dinner.

The town had the animation of a day without sun; vacationers shopped or wandered around wasting time. I came upon a toy store along the seafront and remembered the idea of buying some clothes for the doll, since for that day, at least, I would keep her with me.

I went in with no particular aim, and talked to a young salesgirl, who was very helpful. She found underpants, socks, shoes, and a blue dress that seemed to me the right size. I was about to leave, having just put the package in my bag, when I almost bumped into Corrado, the old man with the spiteful expression, the one who I had been sure was Nina's father and who instead was Rosaria's husband. He was fully dressed, in a blue suit, white shirt, yellow tie. He didn't seem to recognize me, but behind him, in faded green maternity overalls, was Rosaria, who recognized me right away and exclaimed:

"Signora Leda, how are you, is everything all right, did the ointment help?"

I thanked her again, saying I felt fine now, and meanwhile I observed, with pleasure, I should say with emotion, that Nina, too, was coming.

People we are used to seeing on the beach have a surprising effect when we meet them in their city clothes. Corrado and Rosaria seemed to me contracted, rigid, as if they were cardboard. Nina gave the impression of a delicately colored shell that keeps its soft inner mass—colorless, watchful—tightly locked up. The only one who looked disheveled was Elena, who, clasped in her mother's arms, was sucking her thumb. Although she was wearing a pretty white dress, she gave off a sense of disorder; she must have stained the dress a little while ago with chocolate ice cream—the thumb clenched between her lips had a line of sticky brown saliva on it.

I looked at the child uneasily. Her head was lolling on Nina's shoulder, her nose was running. The doll clothes in my purse seemed to have grown heavier and I thought: this is the right moment, I'll tell her that I have Nani. Instead something twisted violently inside me and I asked with false sympathy:

"How are you, sweetie, did you find your doll?"

She gave a kind of shudder of rage, she took her thumb out of her mouth, and tried to hit me with her fist. I swerved, and she hid her face against her mother's neck in irritation.

"Elena, don't behave like that, answer the lady," Nina reproached her nervously. "Tell her we'll find Nani tomorrow, today we're buying a better doll."

But the child shook her head and Rosaria whispered,

whoever stole her should get brain cancer. She said it as if the being in her belly were also furious because of that affront and so she had the right to feel resentment, a resentment even stronger than Nina's. But Corrado made a sign of disapproval. It's kids' stuff, he said, they like a toy, they take it, and then they tell their parents they found it by chance. When I saw him so close he seemed to me not at all old and certainly not as spiteful as he had from a distance.

"Carruno's children aren't like kids," Rosaria said.

And Nina burst out, the accent of her dialect much stronger than usual: "They did it on purpose—they were egged on by their mother to insult me."

"Tonino telephoned, the children didn't take anything."

"Carruno's lying."

"Even if it's true, you are wrong to say it," Corrado reproached her. "What would your husband say if he heard you?"

Nina looked at the pavement angrily. Rosaria shook her head, she turned to me in search of understanding.

"My husband is too kind, you don't know the tears this poor child has shed. She has a fever—we're furious."

I got a confused idea that they had attributed to these Carrunos, probably the family in the motorboat, the doll's disappearance. It was natural for them to think that they had decided to make them suffer by making the little girl suffer.

"The child is having trouble breathing, blow your nose, sweetie," Rosaria said to Elena, and at the same time asked for Kleenex but wordlessly, with a peremptory gesture of her hand. I was opening the zipper of my purse, but stopped abruptly, halfway, afraid that they might see my purchase, ask questions. Her husband quickly gave her a handkerchief and she cleaned the child's nose as she wriggled and kicked. I zipped up my purse, made sure it was tightly closed, and looked at the salesgirl with apprehension. Stupid fears, I was angry with myself. I asked Nina: "Is it a high fever?"

"A few degrees," she answered. "It's nothing." And, as if to show me that Elena was fine, she tried with a forced smile to put her down.

The child refused with great energy. She clung to her mother's neck as if she were suspended over an abyss, yelling, pushing off the floor at the slightest contact, kicking. Nina remained for a moment in an uncomfortable position, bending forward, with her hands around her daughter's hips, pulling in the attempt to detach her, but careful also to avoid her kicks. I felt that she was wavering between patience and being fed up, understanding and the wish to start crying. Where was the idyll I had witnessed at the beach. I recognized the vexation of finding oneself under the eyes of strangers in this situation. Evidently she had been trying to calm the child for hours, without success, and was exhausted. Leaving the house, she had tried to clothe her daughter's rage in a pretty dress, pretty shoes. She herself had put on a nice dress of a wine color that became her, she had pinned up her hair, wore earrings that grazed her pronounced jaw and swung against her long neck. She wanted to resist ugliness, cheer herself up. She had tried to see herself in the mirror as she had been before bringing that organism into the world, before condemning herself forever to adding it on to hers. But to what purpose.

Soon she'll start yelling, I thought, soon she'll hit her,

trying to break that bond. Instead, the bond will become more twisted, will strengthen in remorse, in the humiliation of having shown herself in public to be an unaffectionate mother, not the mother of church or the Sunday supplements. Elena screams, cries, and holds her legs neurotically rigid, as if the entrance to the toy store were a snake pit. A miniature, made of an illogically animate material. The child didn't want to stand on her own feet, she wanted to stay on her mother's. She was apprehensive, she had a presentiment that Nina had had enough, she sensed it from the way she had dressed up to come to town, from the rebellious odor of her youth, from her eager beauty. So she wrapped herself around her. The loss of the doll is an excuse, I said to myself. Elena was afraid, above all, that her mother would flee from her.

Maybe Nina realized it, too, or simply couldn't stand it anymore. In a suddenly coarse dialect she hissed, Stop it, and resettled her daughter in her arms with a violent jerk, Stop it, I don't want to hear you anymore, do you understand, I don't want to hear you anymore, that's enough of your demands, and she pulled the child's dress down hard in front, over her knees, in a sharp gesture that she would have liked to aim at her body, not her clothes. Then, confused, she returned to Italian with an expression of self-reproach, and said to me in a forced way:

"Excuse me, I don't know what to do, she's torturing me. Her father's gone and now she's taking it out on me."

Then, with a sigh, Rosaria took the child from her arms: come to auntie, she murmured, with emotion. This time Elena, incongruously, put up no resistance; she yielded immediately, throwing her arms around her aunt's neck. Out of spite for her mother, or out of certainty that this other body—without a child but expecting one, children love the not yet born a lot, the newborn little, or very little—was at this moment welcoming, would hug her between large breasts, having set her on that stomach, like a seat, protecting her against the possible anger of the bad mother, who didn't know how to take care of her doll, who in fact had lost her. She entrusted herself to Rosaria with a vehement exaggeration of affection, to imply treacherously: Auntie is better than you, Mama, Auntie is kinder; if you go on treating me this way, I'll stay with her forever and won't want you anymore.

"There, go on, so I can have a little rest," Nina said with a frown of disappointment; her upper lip showed a veil of sweat. Then to me: "Sometimes you just can't cope anymore."

"I know," I said, to indicate that I was on her side.

But Rosaria intervened, and, hugging the child, she murmured: they put us through so much, and she planted noisy kisses on Elena, murmuring repeatedly, in a voice consumed by tenderness: pretty girl, pretty pretty girl. Already she wanted to enter the circle of us mothers. She thought that she had waited too long, but that by now she had learned the part completely. In fact she had decided to show immediately, especially to me, that she could soothe Elena better than her sister-in-law. So, here, she set her down on the ground, be a good girl, let Mama and Signora Leda see how good you are. And the child said nothing; she stood beside her sucking her thumb in desperation, while Rosaria asked me, with an air of satisfaction: what were your daughters like as children, were they like this little treasure? I felt a strong impulse to confuse her, to punish her, throw her off balance.

"I remember very little, nothing really."

"That can't be—you don't forget anything about your children."

I was silent for a moment, then said calmly:

"I left. I abandoned them when the older was six and the younger four."

"What do you mean, who did they grow up with?"

"With their father."

"And you didn't see them again?"

"Three years later I took them back."

"What a terrible thing, why."

I shook my head, I didn't know why.

"I was very tired," I said.

Then I turned to Nina, who now looked at me as if she had never seen me: "Sometimes you have to escape in order not to die."

I smiled at her, I gestured toward Elena:

"Don't buy her anything—forget it, it won't help. She'll find the doll. Goodbye."

I nodded at Rosaria's husband, who seemed to me to have assumed his unpleasant mask, and left the store.

15

Now I was really angry with myself. I never spoke of that period of my life, not even to my sisters, not even to myself. The times I had tried to mention it to Bianca and Marta, together or separately, they had listened to me in distracted silence, had said they remembered nothing, had immediately gone on to speak of something else. Only my former husband, before going to work in Canada, had occasionally begun his remonstrances and resentments from that point; but he was an intelligent and sensitive man, ashamed of his meanness, and he quickly moved on, without insisting. All the more reason, then, to wonder why I had confessed what was so much my own to strangers, people very different from me, who would therefore never be able to understand my reasons, and who surely, at that moment, were speaking ill of me. I couldn't bear it, I couldn't forgive myself, I felt I had been flushed out.

I wandered around the square trying to calm down, but the echo of the words I had uttered, Rosaria's expression and her reproaches, the flash of Nina's pupils prevented me, in fact intensified a constricted anger. Useless to say it wasn't important, who were those two women, when would I ever see them again after this vacation. I realized that if that judgment could help me bring perspective to Rosaria it was of no use with Nina. Her gaze had pulled back abruptly, but without losing me: it had only retreated, as if seeking a distant point, in the depths of her pupils, from which to look at me without risk. That urgent need for distance had wounded me.

I walked indifferently among the venders of all sorts of goods, and meanwhile I pictured her the way I had occasionally seen her in those days, watching from behind as with slow, precise movements she spread lotion on her young legs, her arms, her shoulders, and finally her back, tensely twisting around as far as she could get, so that I had had the desire to get up and say here, I'll do it, let me help you, as, when I was a girl, I had thought of doing with my mother, or as I had done often with my daughters. Suddenly I realized that, day after day, without intending to, I had involved her, from a distance, with alternating and often conflicting feelings, in something that I couldn't decipher, but that was intensely my own. For this reason, too, perhaps, I was now furious. I had instinctively used against Rosaria an obscure moment of my life and had done it to astonish her, even in a certain sense to frighten her; she was a woman who seemed to me disagreeable, treacherous. But in reality I would have liked to speak of these very things with Nina alone, on a different occasion—cautiously, in order to be understood.

Soon it started raining again and I had to take shelter in the building that housed the market, amid sharp odors of fish, basil, oregano, peppers. There, jostled by adults and children who arrived hurrying, laughing, wet from the rain, I began to feel sick. The odors of the market nauseated me, the place seemed increasingly close, I was blazing hot, sweating, and the breeze that came in waves from the outside chilled the sweat, causing moments of vertigo. I gained a spot at the entrance, hemmed in by people watching the water cascade down and children screaming, joyfully frightened by the lightning and the thunder that followed. I settled myself almost on the threshold, so that I would feel only the cool air, and tried to get my nerves under control.

What had I done that was so terrible, in the end. Years earlier, I had been a girl who felt lost, this was true. All the hopes of youth seemed to have been destroyed, I seemed to be falling backward toward my mother, my grandmother, the chain of mute or angry women I came from. Missed opportunities. Ambition was still burning, fed by a young body, by an imagination full of plans, but I felt that my creative passion was cut off more and more thoroughly by the reality of dealings with the universities and the need to exploit opportunities for a possible career. I seemed to be imprisoned in my own head, without the chance to test myself, and I was frustrated.

There had been small alarming episodes, not normal impulses of depression, not a destructiveness expressed symbolically, but something more. Now these events have no before and after, they return to my mind in an order that is always different. One winter afternoon, for example, I was studying in the kitchen; I had been working for months on an essay that, although short, I couldn't manage to finish. Nothing fit together, hypotheses were multiplying in my head, I was afraid that the professor who had encouraged me to write it wouldn't help me publish it, would reject it.

Marta was playing under the table, at my feet. Bianca was sitting next to me, pretending to read and write, imitating my gestures, my frowns. I don't know what happened. Maybe she had said something to me and I hadn't responded; maybe she only wanted to start one of her games, which were always a little rough; suddenly, while I was distracted by a search for words that never seemed logical enough, or apt, I felt a slap on the ear.

It wasn't a hard blow, Bianca was five, she couldn't really hurt me. But I was startled, I felt a burning pain, it was as if a sharp black line had, with a clean stroke, cut off thoughts that were already hard to maintain—that were very distant from the kitchen where we were sitting, from the sauce for dinner that was bubbling on the stove, from the clock that was advancing, consuming the narrow space of time that I had to devote to my desire for research, invention, approval, position, money of my own to spend.

I hit the child without thinking about it, in a flash, not hard, my fingertips barely touching her cheek.

Don't do that, I said in a pseudo pedantic tone, and she, smiling, tried to hit me again, certain that at last a game had begun. But I was first and hit her, a little harder, don't you dare ever again, Bianca, and she laughed, hoarsely this time, with a faint bewilderment in her eyes, and I hit her again, still with the tips of my outstretched fingers, again and again, you don't hit Mama, you must never do that, and when, finally, she realized that I wasn't playing, she began to cry desperately.

I feel the child's tears under my fingertips, I'm still hitting her. I do it gently, the gesture is under my control but decisive, and the intervals are getting smaller: not a possibly educational act but real violence, contained but real. Out, I tell her without raising my voice, out, Mama has to work, and I take her solidly by the arm, drag her into the hall, she cries, screams, tries again to hit me, and I leave her there and close the door behind me with a firm shove, I don't want to see you anymore.

The door had a big pane of frosted glass. I don't know what happened, maybe I pushed it with too much force: it banged shut and the glass shattered. Bianca appeared, wide-eyed, small, beyond the empty rectangle, no longer screaming. I looked at her in terror, how far could I go, I frightened myself. She was motionless, unharmed, the tears continued to flow but silently. I try never to think of that moment, of Marta who was pulling me by the skirt, of the child in the hall staring at me amid the broken glass: thinking of it gives me a cold sweat, takes my breath away. I'm sweating here, too, at the entrance of the market, I'm suffocating, and I can't control the pounding of my heart.

16

As soon as the rain slackened, I rushed out, covering my head with my purse. I didn't know where to go, certainly I didn't want to go home. A vacation at the beach, what does it amount to, in the rain: asphalt and puddles, clothes that are too light, wet feet in shoes that give no protection. In the end it was a gentle rain. I was about to cross the street but I stopped. On the sidewalk opposite I saw Rosaria, Corrado, Nina with the child in her arms covered by a thin scarf. They had just left the toy store and were walking quickly. Rosaria was holding by the waist, like a bundle, a new doll that looked like a real child. They didn't see me or pretended not to. I followed Nina with my eyes, hoping she would turn.

The sun began to filter through small blue rents in the clouds. I reached my car, started the engine, drove toward the sea. Faces flashed through my mind, and actions: no words. They appeared, disappeared, there wasn't time to fix anything into a thought. I pressed my fingers against my chest to slow the rapid beating of my heart, and as if to slow the car down as well. I seemed to be going too fast, though in reality I wasn't even going forty. One never knows where the velocity of bad feeling comes from, how it advances. We were at the beach: Gianni, my husband, a colleague of his named Matteo, and Lucilla, his wife, a very cultured woman. I no longer remember what she did in life, I know only that she often caused trouble for me with the children. In general she was kind, understanding, she didn't criticize me, she wasn't mean. But she couldn't resist the desire to seduce my daughters, to make herself loved by them in an exclusive way, to prove that she had a pure and innocent heart—so she said—that beat in unison with theirs.

Like Rosaria. Differences in culture, in class count for little in these things. Whenever Matteo and Lucilla came to our house, or we took a trip outside the city or—as happened in that case—we went on a vacation together, I lived in a state of anxiety, my unhappiness increased. The two men talked about their work or about soccer or I don't know what, but Lucilla never spoke to me, I didn't interest her. She played with the children instead, monopolizing their attention, inventing games just for them, and joining in as if she were their age.

I saw that she was completely intent on the goal of winning them over. She stopped devoting herself to them only when they had given in completely, eager to spend not an hour or two but their whole life with her. She acted like a child in a way that irritated me. I had brought up my daughters not to use babyish voices or coy manners, whereas Lucilla had many affectations; she was, for example, one of those women who purposely speak in the voice that adults attribute to children. She spoke in artificial tones and induced them to do likewise, drawing them into a form of regression first verbal and then, slowly, in all their behavior. Habits of autonomy, which had been imposed by me with difficulty and were necessary to carve out a little time for myself, on her arrival were swept away in a few moments. She showed up and immediately began to play the sensitive, imaginative, always cheerful, always available mother: the good mother. Damn her. I drove without avoiding the puddles, in fact I hit them on purpose, raising long wings of water.

All the rage of that time was returning to my breast.

Easy, I thought. For an hour or two—taking a walk, on a vacation, on a visit—it was simple and pleasant to entertain the children. Lucilla never worried about afterward. She swept away my discipline and then, once the territory that belonged to me was devastated, retreated into hers, devoting herself to her husband, hurrying off to her work, to her successes, of which, among other things, she did nothing but boast in a tone of apparent modesty. In the end I was alone, in permanent service, the bad mother. I remained to tidy up the messy house, to reimpose on the children behavior that they now found intolerable. Aunt Lucilla said, Aunt Lucilla let us do. Damn her, damn her.

Sometimes, but seldom and just barely, I had a small, fleeting taste of revenge. It might happen, for example, that Lucilla arrived at the wrong moment, when the two little sisters were involved in their game, so involved that Aunt Lucilla's games either had to be openly put off until later or, if imposed, bored them. She put a good face on a bad situation, but inside she was bitter. I felt that she was wounded, as if she really were a companion of theirs who had been excluded, and I have to admit that I was pleased, but I didn't know how to take advantage of it, I've never been able to use an advantage. I immediately softened, maybe deep down I was afraid that her affection for the children would diminish and I was sorry. So, sooner or later, I ended up by saying in a sort of apology: it's that they're used to playing with each other, they have their habits, maybe they're a little too self-sufficient. Then she would recover, say yes, and gradually begin to speak ill of my daughters, to pick out flaws and failings. Bianca was too egotistical, Marta too fragile, one had little imagination, the other too much, the older was dangerously closed in on herself, the younger capricious and spoiled. I listened, my small vindication was already changing tune. I felt that Lucilla was compensating for the children's rejection by looking for a way to humiliate me, as if I were their accomplice. I began to suffer again.

The harm she did me in that period was enormous. Whether she was celebrating herself in the games, or becoming bitter when she was excluded from them, she led me to believe that I had done everything wrong, that I was too full of myself, that I wasn't made to be a mother. Damn, damn, damn her. Certainly I must have felt that when, one time, we were at the beach. It was a morning in July, Lucilla had appropriated Bianca, leaving out Marta. Maybe it was because she was younger, maybe because she considered her stupid, maybe because she got less satisfaction from her, I don't know. She must have said something that made her cry and wounded me. I left the little girl whining near Gianni and Matteo, who were sitting under the umbrella, engrossed in conversation, and I took my towel, spread it out a few steps from the sea, and lay down, exasperated, in the sun. But Marta came over to me, she was two and a half, three, she trotted over to play and lay down, all sandy, on my stomach. I hate getting covered with sand, I hate my things getting dirty. I called to my husband to come and get the child. He hurried over, aware that my nerves were on edge; he feared my scenes because he perceived them as uncontrollable. For a while I had made no distinctions between public areas and private ones, I didn't care if people heard me and judged me, I felt a strong desire to act out my rage as if in the theater. Take her, I cried, I can't bear her any longer. I don't know why I was so annoyed with Marta, poor little thing—if Lucilla had been mean to her I should have protected her, but it was as if I believed that woman's reproaches, they made me angry and yet I believed them: as if the child really were stupid, and always whining—I couldn't take it anymore.

Gianni picked her up, giving me a look that meant calm down. I turned my back on him angrily, dived into the water to get rid of the sand and the heat. When I came out, I saw that he was playing with Bianca and Marta, together with Lucilla. He was laughing, Matteo, too, was approaching; Lucilla had changed her mind, she had decided that now Marta could play, she had decided to show me that it could be done.

The child, I saw, was smiling: she was sniffling, but she was really happy, a moment, two. I felt that I harbored in my belly a destructive energy, and by chance I touched my ear. I discovered that the earring was missing. It wasn't of great value, I liked the earrings but wasn't attached to them. Still, I became agitated, I shouted to my husband that I'd lost an earring; I looked on the towel, it wasn't there, and I shouted louder, I've lost an earring; erupting like a fury into their game, I said to Marta: you see, you've made me lose an earring, I said it to her with hatred, as if she were responsible for something that was extremely serious for me, for my life, and then I turned back, I dug in the sand with my feet, with my hands, my husband came over, Matteo came, they began searching. Only Lucilla continued her game with the children, she kept herself out of it, and kept them out of my discomposure.

Later, at home, I yelled at my husband, in front of Bianca and Marta, saying that I didn't want to see her anymore, that bitch, never, and my husband said all right, in order to live in peace. When I left him he and Lucilla had

an affair. Maybe he hoped that she would leave her husband, that she would take care of the children. But she did
neither of those things. She loved him, yes, of course, but
she remained married and paid no more attention to
Bianca and Marta. I don't know how her life went, if she
still lives with her husband, if she separated and remarried,
if she had children of her own. I no longer know anything
about her. We were girls then, who knows what's become
of her, what she thinks, what she does.

17

I parked, went through the pinewood, dripping with
rain. I came to the dunes. The bath house was deserted,
Gino wasn't there, nor was the manager. The beach, in the
rain, had become a dark craggy crust against which the
whitish slab of the sea gently bumped. I went over to the
Neapolitans' umbrellas and stopped at Nina and Elena's,
where, piled up under the beach chair and the lounger or
stuck in an enormous plastic bag, were the child's many
toys. Chance, I thought, or a silent call, should send Nina
here, by herself. Forget the child, forget everything. Greet
each other without surprise. Unfold two beach chairs, look
at the sea together, describe in tranquility my experience,
our hands touching every so often.

My daughters make a constant effort to be the reverse
of me. They are clever, they are competent, their father is
starting them out on his path. Determined and terrified,
they advance like whirlwinds through the world, they will
manage better than us, their parents. Two years ago, when
I had a presentiment that they would be gone a long time,

I wrote a letter for them in which I recounted in detail how it happened that I had abandoned them. I wanted to explain not my reasons—what were they?—but the impulses that more than fifteen years earlier had sent me away. I made two copies of the letter, one for each, and left them in their rooms. But nothing happened, they never answered, they never said: let's talk about it. Only once, at a slightly bitter allusion on my part, Bianca retorted as she went out the door: lucky you, you have time to write letters.

How foolish to think you can tell your children about yourself before they're at least fifty. To ask to be seen by them as a person and not as a function. To say: I am your history, you begin from me, listen to me, it could be useful to you. Nina, on the other hand—I am not Nina's history, Nina could even see me as a future. Choose for your companion an alien daughter. Look for her, approach her.

I stood there for a while, digging with one foot until I found dry sand. If I had brought the doll, I thought, but without regret, I could have buried her here, under the crust of the wet sand. It would have been perfect, someone would have found her the next day. Elena no, I would have wanted Nina to find her, I would have gone up to her, said: are you happy? But I hadn't brought the doll, hadn't done it, hadn't even thought of it. Instead I had bought Nani a new dress, shoes, another action without meaning. Or, in any case, as for so many little things in my life, a meaning that I can't find. I reached the water's edge, I wanted to walk and tire myself out.

And I did walk for a long time, my purse over my shoulder, sandals in one hand, feet in the water. I met almost no one, only a few pairs of lovers. In the first year of Marta's life I discovered that I no longer loved my husband. A hard year, the baby barely slept and wouldn't let me sleep. Physical tiredness is a magnifying glass. I was too tired to study, to think, to laugh, to cry, to love that man who was too intelligent, too stubbornly involved in his wager with life, too absent. Love requires energy, I had none left. When he began with caresses and kisses, I became anxious, I felt that I was a stimulus abused for his solitary pleasures.

Once I had a very closeup view of what it means to be in love, the powerful and joyous irresponsibility that it unleashes. Gianni is Calabrese; he was born in a small town in the mountains where he still has an old family house. Nothing grand, but the air is pure and the landscape beautiful. We would go there, years ago, with the children, at Christmas and Easter. It was an arduous journey in the car, during which he drove in an absent silence and I had to deal with the whims of Bianca and Marta (they wanted to eat continuously, they demanded toys that were in the trunk, they wanted to pee when they had just done so) or try to distract them with songs. It was spring but winter persisted. Sleet was falling, and it was almost dark. We came upon two cold hitchhikers standing at a rest stop.

Gianni approached them almost by instinct, he's a generous man. I said there's no room, we have the children, how are we going to fit. The two got in, they were English, he graying, in his forties, she surely less than thirty. At first I was hostile, taciturn, it complicated the trip for me, I would have to work even harder to make the children behave. It was mainly my husband who talked, he liked to establish relationships, especially with foreigners. He was cordial, he asked questions without paying much heed to conventions. It came out that the two had abruptly left their jobs (I don't remember what they did) and, along with their jobs, their families: she a young husband, he a wife and three small children. They had been traveling for several months through Europe with very little money. The man said seriously: the important thing is to be together. She agreed, and at a certain point said something to this effect: we are obliged to do so many stupid things from childhood on, thinking they're essential; what happened to us is the only thing that has happened to me since I was born that makes sense.

After that I liked them. When it came to dropping them off, that night, on the side of the highway or at a half-deserted gas pump, because it was time for us to turn toward the interior, I said to my husband: let's take them to our house, it's dark, it's cold, tomorrow we'll drive them to the nearest toll plaza. They had dinner under the intimidated gaze of the children, and I opened an old sofa bed for them. Now I had the impression that together, but also separately, they unleashed a power that expanded visibly and struck me, entering into my veins, lighting up my brain. I began to speak overexcitedly, it seemed to me I had a mass of things to say to them alone. They praised my mastery of the language, my husband introduced me ironically as an extraordinary scholar of contemporary English literature. I defended myself, explained what I was studying specifically; they were both interested in my work, the girl especially—something that never happened.

I was captivated by her, her name was Brenda. I talked to her all evening, imagined myself in her place, free, traveling with an unknown man whom I desired at every moment and by whom at every moment I was desired. Everything starting from zero. No habit, no sensations dulled by predictability. I was I, I produced thoughts not distracted by any concern other than the tangled thread of dreams and desires. No one was wrapped around me anymore despite the cutting of the umbilical cord. In the morning, when they said goodbye, Brenda, who knew a little Italian, asked if I had something of mine I could let her read. Of mine: I savored the formulation—*something of mine*. I gave her a wretched extract of a few pages, a small article published two years earlier. Finally they left; my husband drove them back to the highway.

I tidied the house, sadly, slowly, unmade their bed and, as I imagined Brenda naked, felt a liquid excitement between her legs that was mine. I dreamed, for the first time since I was married—for the first time since the birth of Bianca, of Marta—of saying to the man I had loved, to my daughters: I have to go away. I imagined being taken to the highway by them, by all three, and waving goodbye while they went off, leaving me there.

The image persisted. How long did I sit on the guardrail like Brenda, pretending I was her. One or two years, I think, before I actually left. It was a heavy time. I don't think I ever thought of leaving my daughters. It seemed to me terrible, stupidly egotistical. But I did think of leaving my husband, I was looking for the right moment. You wait, you get tired, you start waiting again. Something will happen and in the meantime you become more and more fed up, perhaps dangerous. I couldn't calm down, not even tiredness calmed me.

God knows how long I had been walking. I looked at my watch, turned back toward the bath house, my ankles aching. The sky was clear, the sun was burning, people were lazily appearing on the beach, some dressed, some in bathing suits. The umbrellas reopened, those strolling along the shore became an interminable procession in celebration of vacation's return.

At a certain point I saw a group of children distributing something to the bathers. When I came up to them I recognized them—they were the Neapolitan kids, Nina's relatives. They were giving out flyers, as though it were a game they were playing; each had a sizable packet of them. One, recognizing me, said: why give it to her. I took the flyer anyway, kept walking, then glanced at it. Nina and Rosaria had done what people do when they lose a cat or dog. At the center of the piece of paper was an ugly photograph of Elena with her doll. In big print there was a cell phone number. A few lines, in a tone meant to be moving, said that the child was very grieved by the loss of her doll. A generous reward was promised to whoever found her. I folded the flyer carefully, and put it in my purse beside Nani's new dress.

18

I went home after dinner, dazed by some bad wine I'd drunk. I passed the bar where Giovanni was sitting outside with his friends. Seeing me, he rose, made a gesture of greeting, held out a glass of wine in invitation. I didn't respond and had no remorse for my discourtesy.

I felt very unhappy. I had a sense of dissolving, as if I, an orderly pile of dust, had been blown about by the wind all day and now was suspended in the air without a shape.

I threw my purse on the sofa, didn't open the door to the terrace, didn't open the windows in the bedroom. I went into the kitchen to get some water, in which I mixed a few drops of a sleeping drug that I took only on the rarest occasions. As I drank I noticed the doll sitting on the table and remembered the dress I had in my bag. I felt ashamed. I grabbed the doll by the head, carried her into the living room, and dropped down on the sofa, holding her on my lap with her stomach down.

She was comical with her big buttocks, her straight back. Let's see if this stuff fits, I said aloud, angrily. I pulled out the dress, the underpants, the socks, the shoes. I tried the dress, measuring it against her body upside-down, the size was right. Tomorrow I would go straight to Nina, I would say to her: look, I found her in the pinewood yesterday evening, and this morning I bought her a dress so you can play with her, you and your daughter. I sighed with dissatisfaction; I left everything on the sofa and was about to get up, but realized that more dark liquid had come out of the doll's mouth and stained my skirt.

I examined her lips, pursed around a small opening. They were of a plastic softer than the rest of the body, and yielded under my fingers. I parted them delicately. The opening widened and the doll smiled, showing me gums and baby teeth. I closed the mouth immediately in revulsion, shook her hard. I could hear the water in her belly, and imagined a stomach filth, a stale, stagnant liquid mixed with sand. This is yours, mother and daughter, I thought, why did I interfere.

I slept deeply. In the morning I put my beach clothes in my bag, with books, notebooks, the dress, the doll, and

retraced the road to the sea. In the car I put on an old
David Bowie album, and listened the whole way to the
same song, "The Man Who Sold the World"; it was a part
of my youth. I crossed the pinewood, which was cool and
damp from the previous day's rain. Every so often, I
noticed the leaflet with the picture of Elena on a tree
trunk. I wanted to laugh. Maybe the surly Corrado would
give me a generous reward.

Gino was very kind, I was happy to see him. He had
already set the lounge chair out to dry in the sun, and he
led me to my umbrella, insisting on carrying my bag, but
not once did he use a tone that was too familiar. An intelligent, discreet boy, who should be helped, pushed to finish his studies. I began to read, but distractedly. Gino, too,
on the beach chair, took out his book and gave me a half
smile, as if to emphasize some kinship.

Nina wasn't there yet, nor was Elena. There were the
children who had distributed the flyers the day before, and
in no order, late and wearily, cousins, brothers, in-laws—
all the relatives appeared. Last—it was almost midday—
came Rosaria and Corrado, she in front, in her bathing
suit, displaying the enormous stomach of a pregnant
woman who does not bow to any diet but carries her belly
with confidence, no fuss, followed by him, in undershirt,
shorts, sandals, at a careless pace.

My agitation returned; my heart was racing. Nina, it
was clear, wasn't coming to the beach, maybe the child was
sick. I stared insistently at Rosaria. She had a grim look,
and never glanced in my direction. I tried to catch Gino's
eye, perhaps he knew something, but I realized that his
place was empty, the book abandoned, open on the chair.

As soon as I saw Rosaria leave the umbrella and move

off alone, legs wide, toward the shore, I joined her. She wasn't happy to see me and did nothing to hide it. She responded to my questions in monosyllables, coldly.

"How's Elena?"

"She has a cold."

"Does she have a fever?"

"Slight."

"And Nina?"

"Nina is with her daughter, as she should be."

"I saw the flyer."

She frowned with disapproval.

"I told my brother it was pointless, fucking waste of time."

She was translating directly from dialect as she spoke. I was on the point of telling her yes, it's pointless, fucking waste of time: I have the doll, now I'll take it to Elena. But her hostile tone dissuaded me, I didn't feel like telling her, I didn't feel like telling anyone in the clan. Today I saw them not as a spectacle to be contemplated, compared painfully to what I remembered of my childhood in Naples; I felt them as my time, my own swampy life, which occasionally I still slipped into. They were just like the relations from whom I had fled as a girl. I couldn't bear them and yet they held me tight, I had them all inside me.

Life can have an ironic geometry. Starting from the age of thirteen or fourteen I had aspired to a bourgeois decorum, proper Italian, a good life, cultured and reflective. Naples had seemed a wave that would drown me. I didn't think the city could contain life forms different from those I had known as a child, violent or sensually lazy, tinged with sentimental vulgarity or obtusely fortified in defense of their own wretched degradation. I didn't even look for them, those forms, in the past or in a possible future. I had run away like a burn victim who, screaming, tears off the burned skin, believing that she is tearing off the burning itself.

What I most feared, when I left my daughters, was that Gianni, out of laziness, revenge, necessity, would take Bianca and Marta to Naples, entrust them to my mother and my relatives. I was suffocating with anxiety, I thought: what have I done, I've escaped, but I'm letting them go back there. The two girls would slowly sink into the black well I came from, breathing the habits, the language, all the features I had eliminated from myself when, at eighteen, I left the city to study in Florence, a place that was distant and for me foreign. I had said to Gianni: do what you want but please, don't leave them with their relatives in Naples. Gianni screamed at me that he would do with his daughters what he liked. If I was leaving I had no right to interfere. He took good care of them, in fact, but when he was overwhelmed by work or forced to travel abroad, he took them without hesitation to my mother's house, to the apartment where I was born, the rooms from which I had fought fiercely to free myself, and left them there for months.

The news reached me, I regretted it, but not even for that did I retrace my steps. I was far away; it seemed to me that I was another person, finally the real one, and in the end I let my children be exposed to the wounds of my native city, the ones that in myself I considered incurable. My mother had been wonderful at the time, she had taken care of them, had worn herself out, but I had showed her no gratitude, for that or anything else. The secret rage I harbored against myself I turned on her. Later, when I reclaimed my daughters and brought them to Florence, I accused her of having branded them, as she had branded me. Wicked accusations. She defended herself, she reacted spitefully, extremely upset, and died shortly afterward, perhaps poisoned by her own unhappiness. The last thing she said to me, some time before she died, was, in a fractured dialect, I feel a little cold, Leda, and I'm shitting my pants.

How many things did I scream at her that it would have been better not even to think. I wanted—now that I had come back—my daughters to depend only on me. At times it even seemed to me that I had created them by myself, I no longer remembered anything about Gianni, nothing intimately physical, his legs, his chest, his sex, his taste, as if we had never touched each other. When he went to Canada, that impression hardened, that I had nourished the girls only on myself, that I sensed in them only the female line of my descent, for good and ill. So my anxieties increased. For several years Bianca and Marta did badly in school, obviously they were upset. I got mad at them, pushed them, harassed them. I said: what do you want to do in life, where do you want to end up, do you want to go backward, degrade yourselves, abolish all the efforts your father and I have made, return to being like your grandmother, who got no farther than elementary school. To Bianca I murmured, depressed: I've spoken to your teachers, how you've embarrassed me. I saw them both going off track, they seemed to me more and more pretentious and ignorant. I was sure that they would fail in their studies, in everything, and there was a period when I relaxed only when I knew they had been disciplined; then they began to do well at school, and the shadows of the women of my family vanished.

Poor Mama. In the end what was so terrible about what she passed on to the two girls: nothing, a bit of dialect. Thanks to her, today Bianca and Marta can reproduce the Neapolitan cadence and a few expressions. When they're in a good mood they laugh at me. They exaggerate my accent, even on the telephone, from Canada. They cruelly mock the timbre of the dialect that surfaces from within the way I speak languages, or certain Neapolitan formulations that I use, Italianizing them. Fucking waste of time. I smile at Rosaria, I search for something to say, I expect good manners even if she hasn't any. Yes, my daughters humiliate me, especially with English, they are ashamed of the way I speak; I realized it when we went abroad together. And yet it is the language of my profession, it seemed to me that my use of it was unexceptionable. They, however, insist that I'm not very good, and they're right. In fact, despite my breaking away, I haven't gone very far. If I wanted, in a moment I could go back to being just like this woman, Rosaria. Certainly, it would take some doing; my mother could pass without interruption from the fiction of the petit bourgeois lady to the tormented surge of her unhappiness. I would have to work harder, but I could manage it. The two girls, on the other hand—they've gone far away. They belong to another time, I've lost them to the future.

I smile again, embarrassed, but Rosaria doesn't smile back at me, the conversation ends. I hesitate, now, between a frightened aversion toward this woman and a sad sympathy. I imagine she'll give birth without strain, in two hours she'll expel herself and, at the same time, another just like her. The next day she'll be on her feet, she'll have plenty of milk, a river of nourishing milk, she'll return to battle, vigilant and violent. It's clear to me, now, that she doesn't want

me to see her sister-in-law, she considers her—I imagine—
a pain in the ass who puts on airs, a sissy who during her
own pregnancy was always complaining, throwing up.
Nina to her is soft, liquid, open to all kinds of bad influ-
ences, and I, after my brutal confession, am no longer considered a good friend from the beach. So she wants to protect her from me, afraid I'll put ideas in her head. She keeps
watch in the name of her brother, the man with the slashed
stomach. Bad people, Gino had told me. I was still standing with my feet in the water, I didn't know what to say to
her. Like a magnet, the present—yesterday, today—was
drawing to itself all the past days of my life. I went back to
my umbrella.

I thought about what to do, finally decided. I took my
purse, my shoes, wrapped a pareo around my waist, and
went off toward the pinewood, leaving my books on the
lounge chair, and hanging my dress on the spokes of the
umbrella.

Gino had said that the Neapolitans were staying in a
villa in the dunes, in the shelter of the pines. I followed the
borderline between needles and sand, in shade, in sun.
Soon I saw the villa, a garish two-story structure set among
reeds, oleanders, and eucalyptus. The cicadas at that hour
were deafening.

I headed into the underbrush, looking for a path that
would lead to the house. Meanwhile I took the flyer out of
my purse, and called the cell-phone number that was indi-
cated on it. I waited, hoping that Nina would answer.
While the telephone rang in vain, I heard the querulous
trill of a cell phone in the thick scrub, on my right, and
then the voice of Nina, who was laughing: come on, that's
enough, stop it, let me answer.

I ended the call abruptly, and looked in the direction the voice was coming from. I saw Nina in a thin dress of a pale color, leaning against the trunk of a tree. Gino was kissing her. She seemed to accept the kiss, but with her eyes open, amused, alarmed, as she gently pushed away the hand that was seeking her breast.

19

I went swimming and then lay with my back in the sun, my face between my arms. From that position I could see the boy returning, descending the dunes with long strides, his head down. Back in his place, he tried to read but couldn't, and stared at the sea for a long time. I felt the slight irritation of the evening before turning into hostility. He had seemed so polite, had kept me company for hours, appeared considerate, sensitive. He'd said he was afraid of the fierce reactions of the relatives, of Nina's husband, had put me on my guard. And yet he couldn't contain himself, exposing himself and her to who knows what risks. He tempted her, attracted her just when she was most fragile, crushed by the weight of her daughter. As I had discovered them, they could be discovered by anyone. I felt unhappy with them both.

Surprising them had caused me, I don't know how to put it, distress. It was a confused emotion, adding the seen to the not seen, making me go hot and sweatily cold. Their kiss still burned, warmed my stomach, my mouth had a taste of warm saliva. It wasn't an adult sensation but a childish one, I'd felt like a frightened child. Distant fantasies returned, false, invented images, as when in childhood I'd imagined that my mother secretly left the house, day and night, to meet her lovers, and felt in my body the joy that was hers. Now it seemed to me that an encrusted sediment that had been lying for decades in the pit of my stomach was stirring.

I left my lounge chair nervously, and hurried to gather up my things. I was wrong, I said to myself, Bianca and Marta's departure hasn't been good for me. It seemed so, but it's not. How long has it been since I called, I must hear their voices. Losing your anchor, feeling yourself to be light is not an advantage, it's cruel to yourself and to others. I have to find a way to tell Nina. What's the sense of a summer flirtation, as if you were a sixteen-year-old, while your daughter is sick. She had seemed so extraordinary to me, when she was with Elena, with the doll, under the umbrella, in the sun, or at the water's edge. Often they took turns digging up wet sand with an ice-cream spoon and pretended to feed Nani. How well they got on together. Elena played for hours, alone or with her mother, and you could see that she was happy. It occurred to me that there was more erotic power in her relationship with the doll, there beside Nina, than in all the eros that she would feel as she grew up and grew older. I left the beach without looking even once in Gino's direction, or Rosaria's.

I drove home on the deserted road, my head full of images and voices. When I went back to my children—a long time ago now—the days became heavy again, sex a sporadic and therefore quiet practice, without expectations. Men, even before exchanging a kiss, made it clear to me, with polite conviction, that they had no intention of leaving their wives, or that they had the habits of a bachelor and wouldn't give them up, or that they ruled out taking responsibility for my life and that of my daughters. I never complained; in fact it seemed to me predictable and therefore reasonable. I had decided that the season of passions was over, three years was enough.

Yet that morning when I stripped the bed where Brenda and her lover had slept, when I opened the windows to get rid of their odor, I had seemed to discover in my body a call for pleasure that had nothing to do with that of my early sexual experiences, at the age of sixteen, with the uncomfortable and unsatisfying sex with my future husband, with our conjugal habits before and especially after the birth of the children. After that encounter with Brenda and her man, new expectations arose. I felt for the first time, like a fist in my chest, that I needed something else, but I felt uneasy saying it to myself, it seemed to me that such thoughts were not appropriate for my situation, for the ambitions of a reasonable and educated woman.

Days passed, weeks, the traces of the two lovers faded for good. But I couldn't settle down; instead, a kind of disorder took over my imagination. With my husband I was silent; I never tried to violate our sexual habits, not even the erotic slang we had elaborated over the years. But as I studied, did the shopping, stood in line to pay a bill, I would become lost in desires that embarrassed and at the same time excited me. I was ashamed of them, especially when they intervened while I was taking care of the children. I sang songs with them, read them fables before they fell asleep, helped Marta eat, washed them, dressed them, and meanwhile I felt unworthy, I couldn't figure out how to calm myself.

One morning my professor called from the university

and said that he had been invited to an international con-
ference on E. M. Forster. He advised me to go, it was my
subject, he thought it would be very useful for my work.
What work, I wasn't doing anything, nor had he done
much to smooth the way for me. I thanked him. I didn't
have the money, I had nothing to wear, my husband was
going through a rough period and was very busy. After
days and days of anxiety and depression, I decided I
wouldn't go. But the professor seemed displeased. He said
I was wasting myself. I got angry, and didn't hear from him
for a while. When I heard from him again, he told me that
he had found money to pay for the trip and the hotel.

I had no more excuses. I organized every minute of the
four days I would be gone: food ready in the refrigerator,
visits from girlfriends happy to do all they could for a
slightly mad scientist, a depressed student ready to babysit
the children if their father had unexpected meetings. I
departed, leaving everything in scrupulous order, except
that Marta had a slight cold.

The plane to London was full of well known young aca-
demics, my rivals, who in general had been much more
aggressive and active than I in the race to find a job. The
professor who had invited me was reserved, brooding, a
gruff man. He had two grown children, a kind and gra-
cious wife, a lot of teaching experience, was highly cultured; yet he was seized by panic attacks when he had to
speak in public. During the flight all he did was revise his
paper, and as soon as we were in the hotel he asked me to
read it to see if it was persuasive. I read it, said it was wonderful, soothed him—that was my function. He hurried
off and I didn't see him for the whole first morning. He
appeared only in the late afternoon, just in time to give his

paper. He read the text smoothly, in English, but when there was some criticism, he was distressed, responded brusquely, and went off to his room; he didn't even come down for dinner. I sat at a table with other participants like me, hardly saying a word.

I saw him again the next day. There was an eagerly awaited paper, given by Professor Hardy, an esteemed scholar at a prestigious university. My professor didn't even greet me; he was with others. I found a place at the back of the hall, diligently opened my notebook. Hardy appeared: a man in his fifties, short, thin, with a nice face and extraordinarily blue eyes. He had a low, enveloping voice, and after a while I was surprised to find myself wondering if I would like to be touched by him, caressed, kissed. He spoke for ten minutes, then suddenly, as if his voice were coming from within my erotic hallucination and not the microphone through which he was speaking, I heard him pronounce my name, then my last name.

I couldn't believe it, I felt myself blushing bright red. He went on; he was a skillful speaker, using the written text as a guide, and now improvising. He repeated my name one, two, three times. I saw that my colleagues from the university were looking for me throughout the hall, I was trembling, my hands were sweaty. Even my professor turned with a look of astonishment; I exchanged a glance with him. This English professor was citing a passage from my article, the only one I had published up to then, the same one I had given long ago to Brenda. He quoted it with admiration, he discussed a passage minutely, he used it to better articulate his own argument. I left the hall as soon as he finished his talk and the applause began.

I ran to my room, feeling as if all the liquids inside me

were boiling up under my skin; I was filled with pride. I called my husband in Florence. I almost shouted to him, on the telephone, the incredible thing that had happened to me. He said yes, wonderful, I'm pleased, and told me that Marta had chicken pox, it was definite, the doctor had said there was no doubt. I hung up. Marta's chicken pox sought a space inside me with the usual wave of anxiety, but instead of the emptiness of the past years, it found a joyous future, a sense of power, a blissful confusion of intellectual triumph and physical pleasure. What's chicken pox, I thought, Bianca had it, she'll recover. I was overwhelmed by myself. I, I, I: I am this, I can do this, I *must* do this.

My professor called me in my room. We were not on any kind of familiar terms, he was not a friendly man. His voice was hoarse and always sounded slightly annoyed; he had never thought much of me. He was resigned to the pressures of an ambitious graduate student, but without making promises, in general dumping on me the most boring tasks. But on that occasion he spoke to me kindly, got mixed up, muttered compliments for my success. Among other things he said: you'll have to work harder now, try to finish your new essay quickly, another publication is important. I'll tell Hardy how we're working, you'll see, he'll want to meet you. Impossible, I said, who was I. He insisted: I'm sure.

At lunch he had me sit beside him, and I suddenly realized, with a new wave of pleasure, that everything around me had changed. From anonymous graduate student, without even the right to give a short paper at the end of the day, I had become in the space of an hour a young scholar with some slight international fame. The Italians came one by one to congratulate me, young and old. Then some of the others. Finally Hardy came into the room, someone whispered to him and gestured toward the table where I was sitting. He looked at me for a moment, headed toward his table, stopped, turned back, and came over to introduce himself. Introduce himself to me, politely.

Afterward, my professor said in my ear: he's a serious scholar; but he works a lot, he's getting old, bored. And he added: if you had been male, or ugly, or old, he would have expected you to come to him and offer the proper homage, and then would have dismissed you with some coldly courteous phrase. This seemed to me spiteful. When he made malicious allusions to the hypothesis that Hardy would certainly renew his pursuit that evening I murmured: maybe he's really interested in my contribution. He didn't answer, then said yes, and made no comments when I said, beside myself with joy, that Professor Hardy had invited me to sit at his table at dinner.

I dined with Hardy; I was clever and confident, I drank a lot. Afterward we took a long walk and on the way back, it was two o'clock, he asked me to come to his room. He did it with wit and tact, in an undertone, and I accepted. I had always considered sex an ultimate sticky reality, the least mediated contact possible with another body. Instead, after that experience, I was convinced that sex is an extreme product of the imagination. The greater the pleasure, the more the other is only a dream, a nocturnal reaction of belly, breasts, mouth, anus—of every isolated inch of skin—to the caresses and thrusts of a vague entity definable according to the necessities of the moment. God knows what I put into that encounter, and it seemed to me that I had always loved that man—even though I had just met him—and desired no other but him.

Gianni, when I got home, reproached me because in four days I had called only twice, even though Marta was sick. I said: I had a lot to do. I also said that, after what had happened, I would have to work very hard to take advantage of it. I began to go to the university, provocatively, ten hours a day. When we returned to Florence, my professor, suddenly available, did all he could to help me finish and publish a new essay, and he collaborated energetically with Hardy to enable me to spend some time at his university. I entered a period of painful, frenzied activity. I studied intensely and yet I suffered, because it seemed to me that I couldn't live without Hardy. I wrote him long letters, called him. If Gianni, especially on the weekends, was home, I hurried to a pay phone, dragging Bianca and Marta with me so that he wouldn't become suspicious. Bianca listened to the phone calls and, although they were in English, understood everything without understanding, and I knew it, but I didn't know what to do. The children were there with me, mute and bewildered: I never forgot it, I will never forget it. Yet I radiated pleasure against my own will, I whispered affectionate words, I responded to obscene allusions and made obscene allusions in turn. I was careful—when they pulled me by the skirt, when they said they were hungry or wanted an ice cream or insisted on a balloon from the man with balloons who was just over there—never to say, That's it, I'm leaving, you'll never see me again, as my mother had when she was desperate. She never left us, despite crying that she would; I, on the other hand, left my daughters almost without announcing it.

I drove as if I were not at the wheel, unaware even of the road. Through the windows came a hot wind. I parked at the apartment, I had Bianca and Marta before my eyes, frightened, small, as they had been eighteen years earlier. I was burning hot, and got in the shower immediately. Cold water. I let it run over me for a long time, staring at the sand that slid black down my legs, my feet, onto the white enamel of the floor. The chill of the crooked wing falls down along my body. Get dry, dressed. I had taught that line of Auden's to my daughters, we used it as our private phrase to say that we didn't like a place or that we were in a bad mood or simply that it was a freezing cold day. Poor girls, forced to be cultured even in their family lexicon, from the time they were children. I took my bag, carried it out onto the terrace in the sun, spilled the contents onto the table. The doll fell on one side, I spoke to her, the way one does to a cat or a dog, then I heard my voice and was immediately silent. I decided to take care of Nani, for company, to calm myself. I looked for some alcohol, I wanted to erase the pen marks she had on her face and body. I rubbed her carefully, but I didn't do a good job. Nani, come, dear. Let's put on the underpants, the socks, the shoes. Let's put on the dress. How nice you look. I was surprised by that nickname, which I myself was now easily calling her. Why, among the many that Elena and Nina used, had I chosen that one. I looked in my notebook, I had recorded them all: Neni, Nile, Nilotta, Nanicchia, Nanuccia, Nennella. Nani. You have water in your belly, my love. You keep your liquid darkness in your stomach. I sat in the sun, next to the table, drying my hair, every so often running my fingers through it. The sea was green.

I, too, was hiding many dark things, in silence. The remorse of ingratitude, for example: Brenda. It was she who had given Hardy my text, he told me himself. I don't know how they knew each other, and didn't want to know what reciprocal debts they had. Today I know only that my pages would never have gotten any attention without Brenda. But at the time I told no one, not even Gianni, not even my professor, and above all I never looked for her. It's something that I admitted only in the letter to the girls two years ago, the one they never read. I wrote: I needed to believe that I had done everything alone. I wanted, with increasing intensity, to feel myself, my talents, the autonomy of my abilities.

Meanwhile things were happening in a chain reaction, seemingly the confirmation of what I had always hoped for. I was good; I didn't need to pretend a kind of superiority, as my mother did; I really was a creature out of the ordinary. My professor in Florence was finally sure of it. The famous, sophisticated Professor Hardy was sure of it, he seemed to believe it more than anyone. I left for England, I returned, I left again. My husband was alarmed, what was happening. He protested that he couldn't keep up with work and the children both. I told him that I was leaving him. He didn't understand, he thought I was depressed, he looked for solutions, called my mother, cried that I had to think of the children. I told him that I couldn't live with him any longer, I needed to understand who I was, what were my real possibilities—and other lines like that. I couldn't announce that I already knew all about myself, I had a thousand new ideas, I was studying, I was loving other men, I was in love with anyone who said I was smart, intelligent, helped me to test myself. He calmed down. For a while he tried to be understanding, then he sensed that I was lying, got angry, moved on to insults. Finally he said do what you want, get out.

He had never really believed that I could go without the children. Instead I left them to him, and was gone for two months; I never called. It was he who hunted me down, from a distance, harassing me. When I returned, I did so only to pack my books and notes, for good.

On that occasion I bought dresses for Bianca and Marta, and brought them as a gift. Small and tender, they wanted help in putting them on. My husband took me aside gently, asked me to try again, began to cry, said he loved me. I said no. We quarreled, and I shut myself in the kitchen. After a while I heard a light knocking. Bianca came in, very serious, followed by her sister, timidly. Bianca took on orange from the tray of fruit, opened a drawer, handed me a knife. I didn't understand, I was running after my own desires, I couldn't wait to escape that house, forget it and forget everything. Make a snake for us, she asked then, for herself and Marta, too, and Marta smiled at me encouragingly. They sat in front of me waiting, they assumed the poses of cool and elegant little ladies, in their new dresses. All right, I said, took the orange, began to cut the peel. The children stared at me. I felt their gazes longing to tame me, but more brilliant was the brightness of the life outside them, new colors, new bodies, new intelligence, a language to possess finally as if it were my true language, and nothing, nothing that seemed to me reconcilable with that domestic space from which they stared at me in expectation. Ah, to make them invisible, to no longer hear the demands of their flesh as commands more pressing, more powerful than those which came from mine. I finished peeling the orange and I left. From that moment, for three years, I didn't see or hear them at all.

20

The buzzer sounded, a violent electric charge that reached the terrace.

I looked at the clock mechanically. It was two in the afternoon, I couldn't imagine anyone in the town who knew me well enough to ring at that hour. Gino, it occurred to me. He knew where I lived, maybe he had come for advice.

The buzzer sounded again, less decisive, shorter. I left the terrace, went to answer.

"Who is it?"

"Giovanni."

I sighed, better him than the words with no outlet in my head, and pressed the button to open the street door. I was barefoot and looked for my sandals, I buttoned my shirt, adjusted my skirt, smoothed my wet hair. At the sound of the bell, I went to the apartment door. He stood before me, sunburned, his white hair carefully combed, a slightly loud shirt, blue pants with an impeccable crease, polished shoes, and a paper-wrapped package in his hand.

"I'll take just a minute of your time."

"Come in."

"I saw the car, I said: the signora has come back already."

"Come in, sit down."

"I don't want to bother you, but if you like fish, this is just caught."

He came in, offered me the package. I closed the door, took his gift, made an effort to smile, and said:

"You are very kind."

"Have you had lunch?"

"No."

"You can even eat this raw."

"I would find that disgusting."

"Then fried, and eaten very hot."

"I don't know how to clean it."

He went from being timid to abruptly invasive. He knew the house, he went to the kitchen, began to gut the fish.

"It will take no time," he said. "Two minutes."

I looked at him ironically as with expert motions he removed the guts of that lifeless creature and then scraped away scales as if to take from them their sheen, their color. I thought that probably his friends were waiting at the bar to find out if his undertaking had been successful. I thought that now I had made the mistake of letting him come in and that, if my hypothesis was solid, he would stay, one way or another, long enough to make plausible what he would then recount. Males always have something pathetic about them, at every age. A fragile arrogance, a frightened audacity. I no longer know, today, if they ever aroused in me love or only an affectionate sympathy for their weaknesses. Giovanni, I thought, whatever happened, would boast of his prodigious erection with the stranger, without drugs and despite his age.

"Where do you keep the oil?"

He attended to the frying skillfully, his words tumbling out nervously, as if his thoughts were moving too fast for the structure of the sentences. He praised the past, when there were more fish in the sea and the fish were really good. He spoke of his wife, who had died three years earlier, and his children.

"My oldest son is much older than you."

"I don't think so—I'm old."

"What do you mean old, you're forty at most."

"No."

"Forty-two, forty-three."

"I'm forty-eight, Giovanni, and I have two grownup daughters, one is twenty-four and one twenty-two."

"My son is fifty, I had him at nineteen, and my wife was only seventeen."

"You're sixty-nine?"

"Yes, and three times a grandfather."

"You don't look it."

"All show."

I opened the only bottle of wine I had, a red from the supermarket, and we ate the fish on the table in the living room, sitting beside one another on the couch. It was astonishingly good. I began to talk a lot, feeling reassured by the sound of my voice. I talked about work, about my daughters—mainly about them. I said: they didn't give me many headaches. They were good students, always promoted, they graduated with high marks, they'll become excellent scientists, like their father. They live in Canada now, one is there—more or less—to complete her studies and the older one for work. I'm pleased, I've done my duty as a mother, I've kept them safe from all the dangers of today.

I talked and he listened. Every so often he said something about himself. His older son was a surveyor, his wife worked at the post office; the second, a daughter, had married a good fellow, the one who had the newsstand in the square; the third was his cross, he wouldn't study, made a little money only in the summer, taking tourists out in his boat; the youngest, a daughter, was a bit behind in her studies, she had had a serious illness, but now she was about to graduate from university, she would be the first in the family.

He spoke very sweetly of his grandchildren, they were all his oldest son's, the others no, no children. He created a pleasant atmosphere, and I began to feel at ease, with a sensation of positive attachment to things, the taste of the fish—it was mullet—the glass of wine, the light that radiated from the sea and beat on the glass. He talked about his grandchildren, and I began to talk about my children when they were young. Once, twenty years ago, in the snow, what fun we had had, Bianca and I—she was three, in a pink snowsuit, the hood trimmed with white fur, her cheeks bright red. Dragging our sled, we climbed to the top of a knoll, and then Bianca sat in front, between my legs. I held her tight, and down we went, at top speed, both shouting with joy, and when we got to the bottom the pink of the child's snowsuit had disappeared, and so had the red of her cheeks, hidden under a gleaming layer of ice; only her joyful eyes were visible, and her open mouth saying: again, Mama.

I went on talking and as other happy moments came to mind I felt a longing, not sad but pleasant, for their small bodies, their wish to touch, lick, kiss, hug. Marta would be at the window every day watching for me to come home from work, and as soon as she caught sight of me she couldn't contain herself: opening the door onto the stairs and running down, a soft little body, eager for me, running, so that I was afraid she would fall and gestured to her: slow down, don't run. She was young but agile and confident. I would leave my bag, kneel down, and spread my arms to welcome her. She hurled herself against my body like a bullet, almost knocking me over; I embraced her, she embraced me.

Time goes by, I said, it carries off their little bodies, they remain only in the memory of your arms. They grow, they're as tall as you, they pass you by. Already at sixteen Marta was taller than me. Bianca remained small, her head comes up to my ear. Sometimes they sit in my lap, the way they did when they were little, both talking at once, they caress me, kiss me. I suspect that Marta grew up anxious for me, trying to protect me, as if she were big and I little, and it was this effort that made her so aggrieved, with such a strong feeling of inadequacy. But these are things I'm not sure about. Bianca, for example, is like her father, not demonstrative, but she, too, at times gave me the idea that with her sharp, hard words, orders rather than requests, she wanted to re-educate me for my own good. You know how children are, sometimes they love you by cuddling you, other times by trying to remake you from the start, reinvent you, as if they thought you were badly brought up and they had to teach you how to get on in the world, what music to listen to, what books to read, what films to see, the words you should use and those you shouldn't because they're old now, no one says that anymore.

"They think they know more than we do," Giovanni confirmed.

"Sometimes it's true," I said, "because to what we've taught them they add what they learn outside of us, in their time, which is always different—it's not ours."

"Nastier."

"You think so?"

"We've spoiled them, they expect a lot."

"I don't know."

"When I was a child, what did I have? A wooden gun. A clothespin was fastened to the butt, a rubber band to the barrel. You put a stone in the rubber band the way you do with a slingshot and fastened the stone and the rubber band to the clothespin. So the gun was loaded. When you wanted to shoot, you opened the clothespin and the stone flew off."

I looked at him with sympathy, I was changing my mind. Now he seemed to me a quiet man, I no longer thought he had come to see me so that his companions would think we had had an affair. He was only looking for a little gratification to soften the impact of disappointments. He wanted to talk with a woman who came from Florence, had a nice car, beautiful clothes like the ones on TV, was on vacation alone.

"Today they have everything, people go into debt to buy stupid things. My wife didn't waste a cent, the women of today throw money out the window."

Even that way of complaining about the present and the recent past, and idealizing the distant past, didn't annoy me as it usually does. It seemed, rather, a way, like many, to convince oneself that there is always a slender branch of one's life to hang on to, and, by being suspended there, get used to the inevitability of falling. What would be the sense of arguing with him, telling him: I was part of a wave of new women, I tried to be different from your wife, perhaps also from your daughter, I don't like your past. Why start arguing—better this tranquil lullaby of clichés. At one point he said sadly:

"To keep the children quiet when they were little, my wife would wrap a bit of sugar in a rag for them to suck on."

"A *pupatella*."

"You know it?"

"My grandmother once made one for my younger daughter, who was always crying—no one ever knew what was wrong with her."

"You see? Now they bring them to the doctor, they treat the parents and the children, they think fathers, mothers, and newborns are sick."

While he continued to praise bygone times, I remembered my grandmother. She must then have been more or less the age of this man, I think, but she was small, bent, born in 1916. I had come on a visit to Naples with the two children, tired as usual, angry with my husband who was supposed to come with me and at the last minute had stayed in Florence instead. Marta was crying, she couldn't find her pacifier, my mother reproached me because—she said—I had accustomed my daughter to having that thing in her mouth all the time. I began to quarrel with her, I was fed up, she was always criticizing me. Then my grandmother took a sponge, covered it with sugar, wrapped it in a bit of gauze—from a candy box, I think—and tied a ribbon around it. A tiny being emerged, a ghost in a white robe that hid its body, its feet. I calmed down as if under a spell. Marta, too, in the arms of her great-grandmother, held the white head of that imp in her mouth and stopped crying. Even my mother relaxed, was amused, said that her mother had always quieted me like that: when I was very young and she went out, I would start to cry and scream as soon as she was out of sight.

I smiled, dazed by the wine, and leaned my head against Giovanni's shoulder.

"Do you feel ill?" he asked, embarrassed.

"No, I'm fine."

"Lie down for a while."

I lay on the sofa, and he remained sitting beside me.

"Now it will pass."

"Nothing has to pass, Giovanni, I feel fine," I said gently.

I looked through the window, in the sky there was one cloud, white and slender, and Nani's blue eyes were just visible; she was still sitting on the table, with her rounded forehead, her half-bald head. Bianca I nursed, but Marta wouldn't attach herself: she cried, and I despaired. I wanted to be a good mother, an exemplary mother, but my body refused. I thought of the women of the past, overwhelmed by too many children, of the customs that helped them cure or control the most frantic ones: leaving them alone for a night in the woods, for example, or immersing them in a fountain of freezing water.

"Would you like me to make coffee?"

"No, thank you, stay there, don't move."

I closed my eyes. Nina returned to mind, with her back against the trunk of the tree, I thought of her long neck, her breast. I thought of the nipples that Elena had sucked. I thought of how she hugged the doll against her to show the child how one nurses a baby. I thought of the child who copied the position, the gesture. Yes, they had been lovely, the early days of the vacation. I felt the need to magnify their pleasure in order to get away from my present anguish. In the end what we need above all is kindness, even if it is pretended. I opened my eyes again.

"You've got your color back, you had turned quite pale."

"Sometimes the sea makes me tired."

Giovanni got up, said hesitantly, indicating the terrace:

"If you don't mind, I'll smoke a cigarette."

He went out, lighted a cigarette. I joined him.

"Is it yours?" he asked, pointing to the doll, but like one who wants to say something witty to make himself important.

I nodded yes.

"Her name is Mina, she's my good-luck charm."

He took the doll by the chest, but he was disconcerted, put her down.

"There's water inside."

I said nothing, I didn't know what to say.

He looked at me circumspectly, as if something about me, for a moment, had alarmed him.

"Did you hear," he asked me, "about that poor child whose doll was stolen?"

21

I made myself study, and continued for much of the night. Starting in early adolescence I learned to be extremely disciplined: I chase thoughts out of my head, put pain and humiliation to sleep, push anxieties into a corner.

I stopped around four in the morning. The pain in my back had returned, where the pinecone had hit me. I slept until nine and had breakfast on the terrace, opposite the sea that trembled in the wind. Nani had remained outside, sitting on the table, and her dress was damp. For a fraction of a second it seemed to me that she moved her lips and stuck out the red tip of her tongue, as if playing a game.

I had no desire to go to the beach, I didn't even want to

leave the house. It bothered me to have to pass the bar and see Giovanni chatting with his friends, and yet I felt it was urgent to resolve the matter of the doll. I looked at Nani sadly, caressed her cheek. My unhappiness at losing her had not diminished, in fact it had increased. I was confused; at moments it seemed to me that Elena could do without her, while I could not. On the other hand I had been careless, I had let Giovanni come in without hiding her. I thought for the first time of cutting short my vacation, leaving today, tomorrow. Then I laughed at myself, where was I letting myself go, I was planning to flee as if I had stolen a child and not a doll. I cleaned up, washed, made myself up carefully. I put on a nice dress and went out.

There was a fair going on in the town. The square, the main avenue, the streets and side streets, closed to cars, were a labyrinth of stalls, while the traffic on the edges of town was choked as if it were a city. I mingled with a crowd of mainly women who were rummaging through a huge variety of goods—dresses, jackets, coats, raincoats, hats, scarves, trinkets, household objects of every kind, real or fake antiques, plants, cheeses and salamis, vegetables, fruit, crude marine paintings, miraculous bottles from herbalists. I like fairs, especially the stalls that sell old clothes and the ones with modern antiques. I buy everything, old dresses, shirts, pants, earrings, pins, knickknacks. I stopped to dig among the jumble, a crystal paperweight, an old iron, opera glasses, a metal sea horse, a Neapolitan coffeepot. I was examining a hatpin with a shiny point, dangerously long and sharp, and a beautiful handle of black amber, when my cell phone rang. My daughters, I thought, even if it was an unlikely time. I looked at the display, which showed the name of neither one but a number I seemed to recognize. I answered.

"Signora Leda?"

"Yes."

"I'm the mother of the child who lost the doll, the one that . . ."

I was surprised, I felt anxiety and pleasure, my heart began to race.

"Hello, Nina."

"I wanted to see if this was your number."

"It's mine, yes."

"I saw you yesterday, in the pines."

"I saw you, too."

"I'd like to speak to you."

"All right, tell me when."

"Now."

"Now I'm in town, at the fair."

"I know, I've been following you for ten minutes. But I keep losing you, it's so crowded."

"I'm near the fountain. There's a stall selling old trinkets, I won't move from here."

I pressed my chest, to slow my racing heart. I fingered objects, examined some, but mechanically, without interest. Nina appeared in the crowd, she was pushing Elena in the stroller. Every so often she held on with one hand to the big hat that her husband had given her to keep it from being carried away by the wind from the sea.

"Hello," I said to the child, who had a tired look and the pacifier in her mouth. "Is the fever gone?"

Nina answered for her daughter:

"She's fine, but she won't get over it, she wants her doll."

Elena took the pacifier out of her mouth, and said:

"She has to take her medicine."

"Is Nani sick?"

"She has a baby in her stomach."

I looked at her uncertainly.

"Is her baby sick?"

Nina interrupted with some embarrassment, laughing:

"It's a game. My sister-in-law takes pills and she pretends to give them to the doll, too."

"So Nani is pregnant, too?"

Nina said: "She decided that the aunt and the doll are both expecting a baby. Right, Elena?"

The hat flew off, I picked it up for her. Her hair was pulled up, her face looked more beautiful.

"Thank you, with the wind it won't stay on."

"Wait," I said.

I arranged the hat carefully and used the long pin with the amber handle to fix it in her hair.

"There, it won't fall off. But be careful for the child, disinfect it when you get home, you could easily get a bad scratch."

I asked the man at the stall how much it cost, Nina wanted to pay, I objected.

"It's nothing."

After that she relaxed a little. She complained of the fatigue of recent days, the child had been impossible.

"Come, sweetheart, let's put that pacifier away," she said, "let's not make a bad impression on Leda."

She spoke of her daughter with agitation. She said that ever since Elena had lost the doll she had regressed, she wanted to be either carried or pushed in the stroller, and had even gone back to the pacifier. She looked around, as if searching for a more tranquil spot, and pushed the stroller toward the gardens. She said with a sigh that she was really tired, and she stressed "tired," she wanted me to hear it as not only physical tiredness. Suddenly she burst out laughing, but I understood that she wasn't laughing in fun, there was a bad feeling about it.

"I know you saw me with Gino, but you mustn't think badly of me."

"I don't think badly of anything or anyone."

"Yes, that's obvious. As soon as I saw you, I said to myself: I would like to be like that lady."

"What is it about me in particular?"

"You're beautiful, you're refined, it's clear that you know a great many things."

"I don't really know anything."

She shook her head energetically.

"You have such self-confidence, you're not afraid of anything. I saw it the moment you arrived on the beach for the first time. I looked at you and hoped that you would look in my direction, but you never did."

We wandered a little on the garden paths, and she spoke again of the pinewood, of Gino.

"What you saw has no meaning."

"Now, don't tell lies."

"It's true, I hold him off, and I keep my lips closed. I just want to be a girl again, a little, but pretending."

"How old were you when Elena was born?"

"Nineteen, Elena is almost three."

"Maybe you became a mother too soon."

She shook her head no, insistently.

"I'm happy with Elena, I'm happy with everything. It's just lately, because of these days. If I find the person who is making my child suffer . . ."

"What will you do," I said ironically.

"I know what I'll do."

I caressed one arm lightly as if to tame her. It seemed to me that she was dutifully mimicking the tone and the formulations of her family, she had even accentuated the Neapolitan cadence to be more convincing, and I felt something like tenderness.

"I'm fine," she repeated several times, and told me how she had fallen in love with her husband, she had met him in a discotheque, at sixteen. He loved her, adored her and the daughter. She laughed again, nervously.

"He says my breasts are exactly the size of his hand."

The phrase seemed to me vulgar and I said: "And if he should see you the way I saw you?"

Nina became serious. "He would cut my throat."

I looked at her, at the child. "What do you expect from me?"

She shook her head and murmured: "I don't know. To talk a little. When I see you on the beach I think I would like to sit the whole time under your umbrella and talk. But then you'd be bored, I'm stupid. Gino told me that you're a professor at the university. I was enrolled in literature after high school, but I only took two courses."

"You don't work?"

She laughed again.

"My husband works."

"What does he do?"

She avoided the question with a peevish gesture, and a flash of hostility lighted her eyes. She said: "I don't want to talk about him. Rosaria is doing the shopping, at any moment she might call me and then my time is up."

"She doesn't want you to talk to me?"

She frowned angrily.

"According to her I mustn't do anything."

She was silent for a moment, then she said hesitantly:

"May I ask you a personal question?"

"Let's hear it."

"Why did you leave your daughters?"

I thought, searching for an answer that might help her.

"I loved them too much and it seemed to me that love for them would keep me from becoming myself."

I realized that she was no longer laughing continuously, now she was paying attention to my every word.

"You didn't see them for three years."

I nodded yes.

"And how did you feel without them?"

"Good. It was as if my whole self had crumbled, and the pieces were falling freely in all directions with a sense of contentment."

"You didn't feel sad?"

"No, I was too taken up by my own life. But I had a weight right here, as if I had a stomachache. And my heart skipped a beat whenever I heard a child call Mama."

"You felt bad, then, not good."

"I was like someone who is taking possession of her own life, and feels a host of things at the same time, among them an unbearable absence."

She looked at me with hostility.

"If you felt good why did you go back?"

I chose my words carefully.

"Because I realized that I wasn't capable of creating anything of my own that could truly equal them."

She had a sudden contented smile.

"So you returned for love of your daughters."

"No, I returned for the same reason I left: for love of myself."

She again took offense.

"What do you mean?"

"That I felt more useless and desperate without them than with them."

She tried to dig inside me with her eyes: into my chest, behind my forehead.

"You found what you were looking for and you didn't like it?"

I smiled at her.

"Nina, what I was looking for was a confused tangle of desires and great arrogance. If I had been unlucky it would have taken me my whole life to realize it. But I was lucky and it took only three years. Three years and thirty-six days."

She seemed unsatisfied.

"How did it happen that you decided to go back?"

"One morning I discovered that the only thing I really wanted to do was peel fruit, making a snake, in front of my daughters, and then I began to cry."

"I don't understand."

"If we have time I'll tell you."

She nodded, in an ostentatious way, to let me understand that she would like nothing more than to stay and listen, and meanwhile she realized that Elena had fallen asleep and she gently removed the pacifier, wrapped it in a kleenex, put it in her purse. With a pretty frown she conveyed the tenderness her daughter inspired, and began again:

"And after your return?"

"I was resigned to living very little for myself and a great deal for the two children: gradually I succeeded."

"So it passes," she said.

"What."

She made a gesture to indicate a vertigo but also a feeling of nausea.

"The turmoil."

I remembered my mother and said:

"My mother used another word, she called it a shattering."

She recognized the feeling in the word, and her expression was that of a frightened girl.

"It's true, your heart shatters: you can't bear staying together with yourself and you have certain thoughts you can't say."

Then she asked me again, this time with the mild expression of someone seeking a caress: "Anyway, it passes."

I thought that neither Bianca nor Marta had ever tried to ask me questions like Nina's, and in this insistent tone. I looked for words, in order to lie to her by telling the truth.

"With my mother it became a sort of sickness. But that was another time. Today you can live perfectly well even if it doesn't pass."

I saw her hesitate, she was about to say something else, she stopped. I felt in her a need to hug me, the same need I, too, was feeling. It was an emotion of gratitude that manifested itself as an urgent need for contact.

"I have to go," she said and instinctively kissed me on the lips with a light embarrassed kiss.

When she drew back I saw behind her, at the end of the garden, against the stalls and the crowd, Rosaria and her brother, Nina's husband.

22

I said softly: "Your sister-in-law and your husband are here."

There was a spark of irritated surprise in her eyes but she remained calm, she didn't even turn around.

"My husband?"

"Yes."

Dialect got the upper hand, and she murmured: what the fuck is he doing here, that shit, he was supposed to come tomorrow night, and she pushed the stroller carefully in order not to wake the child.

"May I telephone you?" she asked.

"When you like."

She waved a hand cheerfully in a sign of greeting, her husband waved back.

"Come with me," she said.

I went with her. The two siblings, standing at the entrance to the garden, for the first time struck me with their resemblance. The same height, the same broad face, the same strong neck, the same prominent, fat lower lip. I thought, marveling, that they were handsome: solid bodies firmly planted in the asphalt of the street like plants accustomed to sucking up even the slightest bit of watery fluid. They are strong ships, I said to myself, nothing can hold them back. I, on the other hand, have only restraints. It was the fear I'd had of these people since childhood, and at times disgust, and also my presumption of having a superior destiny, an elevated sensibility, that up to now had kept me from admiring their determination. Where is the rule that makes Nina pretty and Rosaria not. Where is the rule that makes Gino handsome and this threatening husband not. I looked at the pregnant woman and seemed to see, beyond the belly swathed in a yellow dress, the daughter who was feeding on her. I thought of Elena who, worn out, was sleeping in the stroller, of the doll. I wanted to go home.

Nina kissed her husband on the cheek, said in dialect: I'm so happy you came early, and added, when he leaned over to kiss the child: she's sleeping, don't wake her, you know lately she's been tormenting me. Then, indicating me with her hand: you remember the lady, she's the one who found Lenuccia. The man kissed the child softly on the forehead, she's sweaty, he said, also in dialect, sure she doesn't have a fever? And as he rose—I saw the heavy stomach in the shirt—he turned cordially toward me, still in dialect: you're still here, lucky you who have nothing to do, and Rosaria immediately added seriously, but with better control of her words: the signora works, Tonì, she works even when she's swimming, she's not like us, just splashing around, good day, Signora Leda, and they left.

I saw Nina insert an arm under her husband's, she went off without turning even for a moment. She was talking, laughing. It seemed to me that she had been suddenly pushed—too slight as she was, between husband and sister-in-law—to a distance much greater than that which separated me from my daughters.

Outside the fair area was a chaos of cars, raveled streams of adults and children, either moving away from the stalls or converging on them. I went along the deserted streets. I climbed the stairs to my apartment, the last flight with a sensation of urgency.

The doll was still on the table on the terrace, the sun had dried her dress. I undressed her carefully, taking everything off. I recalled that Marta, as a child, had the habit of sticking things in every little hole she found, as if to hide them and be sure of finding them again. Once I came across tiny pieces of uncooked spaghetti in the radio. I took Nani into the bathroom, I held her by the chest with one hand, head down. I shook her hard, dark drops of water trickled from her mouth.

What had Elena put in there. I had been so happy to learn, when I was pregnant the first time, that life was reproducing in me. I wanted to do everything as well as possible. The women of my family swelled, dilated. The creature trapped in their womb seemed a long illness that changed them: even after the birth they were no longer the same. I, instead, wanted my pregnancy to be under control. I was not my grandmother (seven children), I was not my mother (four daughters), I was not my aunts, my cousins. I was different and rebellious. I wanted to carry my inflated belly with pleasure, enjoying the nine months of expecting, scrutinizing the process, guiding and adapting it to my body, as I had stubbornly done with everything in my life from early adolescence. I imagined myself a shining tile in the mosaic of the future. So I was vigilant, I followed the medical prescriptions rigorously. For the duration of the pregnancy I remained attractive, elegant, active, and happy. I talked to the creature in my belly, I had her listen to music, I read to her in the original the texts I was working on, I translated them for her with an inventive effort that filled me with pride. What later became Bianca was for me Bianca right away, a being at its best, purified of humors and blood, humanized, intellectualized, with nothing that could evoke the blind cruelty of live matter as it expands. I managed to vanquish even the long and violent labor pains I suffered, reshaping them as an extreme test, to be confronted with solid preparation, containing the terror, and leaving of myself—and above all to myself—a proud memory.

I did well. How happy I was when Bianca came out of me and, holding her in my arms for a few seconds, I realized that it had been the most intense pleasure of my life. If I look now at Nani with her head down, vomiting into the sink a brown spray mixed with sand, I find no resemblance to my first pregnancy; even the morning sickness was mild and didn't last. But then came Marta. She attacked my body, forcing it to turn on itself, out of control. She immediately manifested herself not as Marta but as a piece of living iron in my stomach. My body became a bloody liquid; suspended in it was a mushy sediment inside which grew a violent polyp, so far from anything human that it reduced me, even though it fed and grew, to rotting matter without life. Nani, with her black spittle, resembles me when I was pregnant for the second time.

I was already unhappy, but I didn't know it. It seemed to me that little Bianca, right after her beautiful birth, had suddenly changed and treacherously taken for herself all my energy, all my strength, all my capacity for imagination. It seemed to me that my husband, too caught up in his fury of accomplishment, didn't notice that his daughter, now that she was born, had become voracious, demanding, hostile as she had never seemed when she was in my stomach. I gradually discovered that I didn't have the strength to make the second experience exalting, like the first. My head sank inside the rest of my body, there seemed no prose, verse, rhetorical figure, musical phrase, film sequence, color capable of taming the dark beast I was carrying in my womb. The real breakdown for me was that: the giving up of any sublimation of my pregnancy, the destruction of the happy memory of the first pregnancy, the first birth.

Nani, Nani. The doll, impassive, continued to vomit. You've emptied all your slime into the sink, good girl. I parted her lips, with one finger held her mouth open, ran some water inside her and then shook her hard to wash out the murky cavity of her trunk, her belly, to finally get the baby out that Elena had put inside her. Games. Tell the girls everything, starting from their childhood: they'll take care, later, of inventing an acceptable world. I myself was playing now, a mother is only a daughter who plays, it was helping me think. I looked for my eyebrow tweezers, there was something in the doll's mouth that wouldn't come out. Begin again from here, I thought, from this thing. I should have noticed right away, as a girl, this soft reddish engorgement that I'm now squeezing with the metal of the tweezers. Accept it for what it is. Poor creature with nothing human about her. Here's the baby that Lenuccia stuck in the stomach of her doll to play at making it pregnant like Aunt Rosaria's. I extracted it carefully. It was a worm from the beach, I don't know what the scientific name is: the ones amateur fishermen find at twilight, digging in the wet sand, as my older cousins did four decades ago, on the beaches between Garigliano and Gaeta. I looked at them then spellbound by my revulsion. They picked up the worms with their fingers and stuck them on the hooks as bait; when the fish bit, the boys freed them from the iron with an expert gesture and tossed them over their shoulders, leaving them to their death agonies on the dry sand.

I held Nani's pliant lips open with my thumb while I

operated carefully with the tweezers. I have a horror of crawling things, but for that clot of humors I felt a naked pity.

23

I went to the beach in the late afternoon. I watched Nina in the distance, from my umbrella, again with the benevolent curiosity of the first days of the vacation. She was anxious, Elena wouldn't leave her for an instant.

At sunset, as they were preparing to go home and the child was screaming that she wanted to go swimming again, and Rosaria intervened, offering to take her to the water, Nina lost her composure and began yelling at her sister-in-law, in a harsh dialect, full of vulgarity, which attracted the attention of the whole beach. Rosaria was silent. Instead Tonino, Nina's husband, interrupted, and dragged her toward the shore, holding her by one arm. He was a man who seemed trained never to lose his composure, not even when his actions become violent. He spoke to Nina firmly but as if in a silent film, not a sound reached me. She stared at the sand, touched her eyes with her fingertips, occasionally said no.

The situation gradually became normal and the family swarmed in groups toward the villa in the pinewood, Nina exchanging cold words with Rosaria, Rosaria carrying Elena, now and again covering her with kisses. I watched Gino tidy up the beach chairs, lounge chairs, abandoned toys. I saw him pick up a blue pareo that had been left hanging on an umbrella and fold it carefully, with absorption. A boy came running back and, barely slowing down, grabbed the pareo rudely, then disappeared toward the dunes.

Time slipped away in a melancholy fashion, the weekend came, with its great influx of beachgoers; already on Friday they were arriving in masses. It was hot. The crowd increased Nina's tension. She watched her daughter obsessively, springing like an animal as soon as she saw her move a few steps. We exchanged brief greetings at the water's edge, a few words about the child. I knelt beside Elena, said to her something in play; her eyes were red and she had mosquito bites on her cheek and forehead. Rosaria came to put her feet in the water, but she ignored me; it was I who said hello and she answered reluctantly.

At one point during the morning I saw that Tonino, Elena, and Nina were having ice cream in the bar at the beach house. I passed by to go to the counter and order a coffee, but it seemed to me that they didn't even see me, they were too taken up by the child. Yet, when I was about to pay, the manager told me that I owed nothing, Tonino had made a sign to put it on his bill. I wanted to thank him, but they had left, and were on the beach with Elena, paying little attention to her, though, for now they were quarreling.

As for Gino, it was enough for me to turn my head every so often to catch him watching them from a distance as he pretended to study. The beach got more and more crowded, Nina mingled among the bathers, but the boy put aside his textbook and began using the binoculars he had been issued, as if he feared from one moment to the next a tidal wave. I thought not so much of what he saw with his eyes empowered by the lenses but of what he imagined: the early hours of the hot afternoon, when the big family of Neapolitans retreated from the sea; the conjugal bed in the half light; Nina bound to the body of her husband, their sweat.

The young mother returned to the beach around five in the afternoon, cheerful, her husband beside her with Elena in his arms, and Gino stared at her, desolate, then hid his gaze in his book. Every so often he turned in my direction but immediately looked away. We were both waiting for the same thing: for the weekend to go by quickly, the beach to become peaceful again; Nina's husband would leave, and she would again be in contact with us.

In the evening I went to the movies, an ordinary film in a half-empty theater. As the lights went out, and the film began, a group of boys came in. They ate popcorn, they laughed, they insulted one another, they tried out the rings of their cell phones, they shouted obscenities at the shadows of the actresses on the screen. I can't bear to be disturbed when I'm watching a movie, even if it's a bad movie. So at first I uttered imperious whispers, then, since they paid no attention, I turned to them and said that if they didn't stop it I would call the usher. They were the boys from the Neapolitan family. Call the usher, they jeered, maybe they had never heard the word. One shouted at me in dialect: go ahead, bitch, why don't you call the dickhead. I got up and went to the ticket window. I explained the situation to a bald man who seemed lazy but kind. He assured me that he would take care of it and so I went back into the theater amid the boys' laughter. A moment later, the man pushed aside the curtain, entered, looked around. Silence. He stood there for a few minutes and then withdrew. Immediately the clamor started up again. The other spectators were silent; I rose and shouted, a little hysterically, I'm going to call the police. They began to sing, in falsetto, *Viva, viva la polizia*. I left.

The next day, Saturday, the little gang was at the beach, they seemed to be waiting for me. They jeered, they pointed, they stared at me, muttering to Rosaria. I thought of appealing to Nina's husband, but I was ashamed of the idea, it seemed to me that I had momentarily entered into the logic of the group. Around two, exasperated by the crowd, by the loud music coming from the beach house, I gathered up my things and left.

The pinewood was deserted, yet soon I felt that I was being followed. The memory of the pinecone that had hit me in the back suddenly returned, and I walked faster. The scuffling sound behind me continued, and, in a panic, I started to run. The noises, the voices, the smothered laughter grew louder. The clamor of the cicadas, the odor of hot resin were no longer pleasant, but seemed a trove of anxiety. I slowed down: not because my fear was lessening but out of dignity.

At the apartment I felt ill, I broke out in a cold sweat, then felt hot, as if I were suffocating. I lay on the couch and slowly calmed down. I tried to rouse myself, and swept the house. The doll was still naked, head down in the bathroom sink, and I dressed her. The water was no longer gurgling in her stomach; I imagined her womb as a dry ditch. Organize, understand. I thought how one opaque action generates others of increasingly pronounced opacity, and so the problem is to break the chain. Elena would be happy to have her doll again, I said to myself. Or no, a child never wants only what it's asking for, in fact a satisfied demand makes even more unbearable the need that has not been confessed.

I took a shower, looked in the mirror as I dried myself. The impression I had had of myself in these months changed abruptly. I wasn't newly youthful but aged, excessively thin, a body so lean as to seem without depth, white hairs in the black of my sex.

I went out, found a drugstore where I could weigh myself. The scale printed out weight and height on a piece of paper. I was three inches shorter and underweight. I tried again and my height diminished further, as did my weight. I went away disoriented. Among my most dreaded fantasies was the idea that I could get smaller, go back to being adolescent, child, condemned to relive those phases of my life. I didn't start liking myself until I turned eighteen, when I left my family, my city, to study in Florence.

I walked along the sea until evening, nibbling fresh coconut, toasted almonds, hazelnuts. The shops were lighted, the young Africans spread their wares on the sidewalks, a fire-eater began to spit out long flames, a clown knotted colored balloons into animal forms, attracting a big audience of children, the Saturday-night throng grew. I discovered that a dancing party was to be held in the square, and I waited for it to begin.

I like dancing, I like to watch people dance. The orchestra started with a tango; it was mainly older couples who ventured out, and they were good. Among the dancers I recognized Giovanni, whose steps and figures had a serious intensity. The spectators multiplied, the circle around the edges of the square expanded. The dancers, too, grew in number, and their competence diminished. Now people of all ages were dancing, polite grandsons with grandmothers, fathers with ten-year-old daughters, old women with old women, children with children, tourists and local people. Suddenly Giovanni was standing in front of me, asking me to dance.

I left my purse with an old woman he knew and we danced, a waltz, I believe. From then on we didn't stop. He talked about the heat, the starry sky, the full moon, and how the mussels were flourishing. I felt better and better. He was sweaty, tense, but he continued to ask me to dance, with true courtesy, and I accepted, I was having a good time. He left me, apologizing, only when, at a certain point, the Neapolitan family appeared in the crowd, at the edge of the square.

I went to get my purse and I observed him as he politely greeted Nina, Rosaria, and finally, with particular deference, Tonino. I also saw him trying clumsily to pet Elena, who, in her mother's arms, was eating a roll of cotton candy twice as big as her face. When the greetings were over, he remained beside them, stiff, uneasy, saying nothing, but as if he were proud to be seen in their company. I understood that for me the evening was over and I prepared to go. But I realized that Nina was handing her daughter to Rosaria and now was forcing her husband to dance. I stayed a little longer to watch her. Her movements had a natural, pleasing harmony, even—or perhaps especially—in the arms of that graceless man. I felt a touch on my arm. It was Gino, who had leaped like a beast from some corner where he had been squatting. He asked if I wanted to dance, I said I was tired, very hot, but at the same time I felt light and gay, and so I took him by the hand and we danced.

I quickly realized that he intended to guide me toward Nina and her husband, wanting her to see us. I helped him, and then I didn't mind being seen in the arms of her suitor. But in the throng of couples it was difficult to reach them and we both gave up without saying anything. I had my purse on my shoulder but, well, all right. It was pleasant to dance with that slender, tall dark boy, with his shining eyes and mussed hair and dry palms. His nearness was so different from Giovanni's. I felt the difference in bodies, in odors. I perceived it as a division in time: it seemed to me that that very evening, there in the square, had been split in half and that I had magically ended up dancing in two different stages of my life. When the music ended, I said I was tired, Gino wanted to take me home. We left the square behind us, the sea walk, the music. We spoke of his exam, of the university. At the door I saw that he was having a hard time saying goodbye.

"Would you like to come up," I asked.

He made a gesture of no, he was embarrassed, he said:

"It's beautiful, the gift you gave Nina."

It irritated me that they had managed to see each other and that she had even showed him the pin. He added:

"She was really grateful for your kindness."

I grumbled a yes, I was pleased. Then he said:

"I have something to ask you."

"What."

He didn't look me in the face, but stared at the wall behind me.

"Nina wants to know if you would be willing to lend us your place for a few hours."

I felt uneasy, a dart of bad humor that poisoned my veins. I looked at the boy to see if that formulation concealed a request not from Nina but born of his own desire. I said sharply:

"Tell Nina I'd like to talk to her."

"When?"

"As soon as she can."

"Her husband leaves tomorrow evening, before that it's impossible."

"Monday morning is fine."

He was silent, now he was nervous and couldn't leave.

"Are you angry?"

"No."

"But you made a face."

I said coldly:

"Gino, the man who takes care of my apartment knows Nina and has business with her husband."

He had an expression of disdain, a half smile.

"Giovanni? He doesn't count. Ten euros and he says nothing."

Then I said to him with a rage that I couldn't conceal: "Why did you decide to ask this of me in particular?"

"Nina wanted it that way."

24

I had a hard time getting to sleep. I thought about calling the girls, they were there, in a corner of my mind, but I kept losing them in the confusion of the days. This time, too, I decided against it. They'll just give me a list of the things they need, I sighed. Marta will say that I went to the trouble of sending Bianca her notes, but forgot something—I don't know what, there's always something—that she'd asked for. It's been like that since they were young, they live in the suspicion that I do more for one than for the other. Once it was toys, candy, even the quantity of kisses dispensed. Afterward they began to argue over clothes, shoes, motorcycles, cars—that is, money. Now I have to pay attention to give one exactly what I give the other, because each, resentful, keeps a secret account. They've felt since childhood that my affection is transient, and so they evaluate it on the basis of the concrete services I provide, the goods I distribute. Sometimes I think they see me now only as a material inheritance that they will have to quarrel over after my death. They don't want the same thing to happen with the money, with our few goods, that, in their view, happened with the transmission of my physical features. No, I don't feel like listening to their complaints. Why don't they call me. If the phone doesn't ring, evidently they don't have urgent demands. I tossed and turned in the bed; I couldn't get to sleep, and was enraged.

In any case, satisfying your daughters' demands is something you accept. In late adolescence, Bianca and Marta, in shifts that were brutally assigned, had asked me a hundred times to leave them the apartment free. They had their sexual dealings and I had always been accommodating. I thought: better at home than in a car, in a dark street, in a field, among a thousand discomforts, exposed to so many risks. So I had gone, with a sigh, to the library or the movies or to sleep at a friend's house. But Nina? Nina was an image on the beach in August, an entanglement of looks and a few words, at most the victim—she and her daughter—of my reckless gesture. Why should I leave her my house, how had it occurred to her.

I got up, wandered around the apartment, went out on the terrace. The night was still echoing with the sounds of the fair. Suddenly, clearly, I felt the thread that stretched between that girl and me: we hardly knew each other, and yet the bond strengthened. Perhaps she wanted me to refuse her the keys, so that she could refuse herself a dangerous outlet for her restlessness. Or she wanted me to give her the keys, so that she could feel in that gesture the authorization to take the risk of flight, the road to a future different from the one that was already written for her. Anyway, she wanted the experience, the wisdom, the rebel force that in her imagination she attributed to me—she wanted me to put these at her service. She needed me to take care of her, to follow her step by step, sustaining her in the choices that, whether I gave her the keys, or refused, I would nevertheless have pushed her to make. It seemed to me, when at last the sea and the town had grown silent, that the problem was not the demand for some hours of love with Gino in my house but her giving herself to me so that I might concern myself with her life. The beam from the lighthouse was, at fixed intervals, casting an unbearable light on the terrace, so I got up and went back inside.

I ate some grapes, in the kitchen. Nani was on the table. She seemed to have a clean fresh look, but also an indecipherable expression, *tohu-bohu*, without the light of a clear order, of a truth. When had Nina chosen me, on the beach. How had I entered her life. By pushes and shoves, certainly; chaotically. I had assigned her the role of perfect mother, of successful daughter, but I had complicated her existence by taking the doll away from Elena. I had seemed to her a free woman, independent, refined, courageous, with no hidden corners, but I had composed my answers to her anxious questions as exercises in reticence. By what right, why. Our similarities were superficial, she ran risks much greater than those I had run twenty years earlier. As a girl I had been endowed with a strong sense of myself, I was ambitious, I had detached myself from my family with the same bold force with which we free ourselves from someone who is tugging on us. I had left my husband and my daughters at a moment when I was sure I had the right, was in the right, not to mention that Gianni, though desperate, hadn't persecuted me, he was a man sensitive to the needs of others. In the three years without my daughters I had never been alone, there was Hardy, a prestigious man, he loved me. I had felt sustained by a small world of friends, men and women who, even when they argued with me, breathed the same culture, understood my ambitions and my depressions. When the weight in the pit of my stomach became unbearable and I went back to Bianca and Marta, some people had silently withdrawn from my life, some doors had been closed forever, my ex-husband had decided that it was his turn to flee and had gone to Canada, but no one had thrown me out, branding me as contemptible. Nina, however, had not even one of the defenses that I had erected before the break. The world in the meantime had not improved; in fact it had become crueler for women. She—she had said—for much less than what I had done years before risked having her throat cut.

I carried the doll to the bedroom. I gave her a pillow to lean against, I settled her on the bed the way people used to do in certain houses in the south, so that she was sitting up, arms spread, and I lay down beside her. I thought of Brenda, the English girl I had met for just a few hours in Calabria, and I realized suddenly that the role Nina was pushing me into was the same I had given her. Brenda had appeared on the highway for Reggio Calabria and I had endowed her with a power that I wanted in my turn to have. She perhaps had realized it and, at a distance, with a minimal gesture, had helped me, leaving me then to take responsibility for my life. I could do the same. I turned off the light.

25

I woke late, ate something, decided not to go to the beach. It was Sunday and the preceding Sunday had left a bad memory. I set myself up on the terrace with my books and notebooks.

I was quite satisfied with the work I was doing. My academic life had never been easy, but recently, certainly through my own fault—over the years my disposition had worsened, I had become obstinate, at times irascible—things had been further complicated, it was urgent that I get back to serious study. The hours ran by without distractions. I worked as long as there was light, disturbed only by the damp heat, some wasps.

While I was watching a TV movie—it was almost midnight—the cell phone rang. I recognized Nina's number, answered. She asked me, all in one breath, if she could come see me tomorrow, at ten in the morning. I gave her the address, turned off the television, and went to bed.

The next day I went out early to have a copy of the keys made. I came back at five minutes before ten, the phone rang while I was still on the stairs. Nina said that ten was impossible, she hoped to be able to come by around six.

She has decided, I thought, she won't come. I prepared my bag for the beach but then decided against it. I didn't

feel like seeing Gino, and the spoiled, violent children of the
Neapolitans annoyed me. I had a shower, put on a two-piece
bathing suit, and lay in the sun on the terrace.

The day slipped by slowly between showers, sun, fruit,
work. Every so often I thought of Nina, looked at the
clock. By summoning her I had made everything more difficult for her. At first she must have counted on the fact
that I would give the keys to Gino and would make an
arrangement with him for the day, the hours when I would
leave the apartment. But from the moment I asked to
speak directly to her, she had begun to hesitate. I imagined
that she didn't feel she could address to me directly a
request for complicity.

But at five, while I was still in my bathing suit, in the
sun, with my hair wet, the buzzer rang. It was she. I waited in the doorway for her to come up the stairs. She
appeared in her new hat, out of breath. I said come in, I
was on the terrace, I'll be dressed in a moment. She shook
her head no, energetically. She had left Elena with Rosaria
with the excuse that she had to go to the pharmacy for
some nose drops that would clear up the child's stuffy
nose. She has trouble breathing, she said, she's always in
the water and has a cold. I felt that she was very agitated.

"Sit down for a moment."

She freed the hat from the pin, she laid both objects on
the table in the living room, and I thought, looking at the
black amber, the long shining shaft, that she had worn the
hat just to show me that she was using my gift.

"It's lovely here," she said.

"Do you really want the keys?"

"If it's all right with you."

We sat on the sofa. I told her I was surprised, I reminded her gently that she had claimed she was happy with her husband and Gino was only a game. She confirmed everything, uneasily. I smiled.

"And so?"

"I can't take it anymore."

I searched for her gaze, she didn't look away, I said all right. I took the keys from my purse, placed them on the table beside the pin and the hat.

She looked at the keys, but she didn't seem happy. She said:

"What do you think of me?"

I took the tone that I usually use with my students.

"I think that this way you're risking everything. You should return to your studies, Nina, graduate and find a job."

She made a grimace of disappointment.

"I know nothing and I'm worth nothing. I got pregnant, I gave birth to a daughter, and I don't even know how I'm made inside. The only true thing I want is to escape."

I sighed.

"Do what you feel you want to do."

"Will you help me?"

"I am."

"Where do you live?"

"Florence."

She laughed in her usual way, nervously.

"I'll come to see you."

"I'll leave you my address."

She was about to take the keys, but I rose and said:

"Wait, I have to give you something else."

She looked at me with a hesitant smile, she must have

thought it was another gift. I went to the bedroom, I took Nani. I came back and she was playing with the keys, she had a half smile on her lips. She looked up, the smile vanished. She said in a stupefied whisper:

"You took her."

I nodded yes and she jumped up, leaving the keys on the table as if they burned her, murmured, "Why?"

"I don't know."

She raised her voice suddenly, said:

"You read, you write all day, and you don't know?"

"No."

She shook her head, incredulous, her voice lowered. "You had her. You kept her, while I had no idea what to do. My daughter was crying, she was driving me mad, and you, you didn't say a word, you saw us but you didn't make a move, you didn't do a thing."

I said: "I'm an unnatural mother."

She agreed, exclaiming yes, you're an unnatural mother, took the doll from my hands with a fierce gesture of reappropriation, to herself she cried in dialect I have to go, and to me in Italian: I don't want to see you anymore, I don't want anything from you, and she went toward the door.

I made a broad gesture, and said:

"Take the keys, Nina. I'm leaving tonight, the house will be empty till the end of the month," and I turned toward the window, I couldn't bear to see her so maddened by rage, I murmured: "I'm sorry."

I didn't hear the door close. For a second I thought she had decided to take the keys, then I heard her behind me, hissing insults in dialect, terrible as the ones my grandmother, my mother used to utter. I was about to turn away, but I felt a pain in my left side, swift as a burn. I looked down and saw the point of the pin that was shooting out of my skin, above my stomach, just under my ribs. The point appeared for a fraction of a second only, the time that Nina's voice lasted, her hot breath, and then disappeared. The girl threw the pin on the floor, she didn't take her hat, didn't take the keys. She ran off with the doll, closing the door behind her.

I leaned one arm against the window and looked at my side, the tiny drop of blood immobile on the skin. I waited for something to happen to me, but nothing did, the drop became dark, clotted, and the impression of the painful thread of fire that had pierced me faded.

I sat down cautiously on the sofa. Maybe the pin had pierced my side the way a sword pierces the body of a Sufi ascetic, doing no harm. I looked at the hat on the table, the crust of blood on the skin. It was dark. I rose and turned on the light. I started to pack my bags, but moving slowly, as if I were gravely injured. When the suitcases were ready, I dressed, put on my sandals, smoothed my hair. At that point the cell phone rang. I saw Marta's name, I felt a great contentment, I answered. She and Bianca, in unison, as if they had prepared the sentence and were performing it, exaggerating my Neapolitan cadence, shouted gaily into my ear:

"Mama, what are you doing, why haven't you called? Won't you at least let us know if you're alive or dead?"

Deeply moved, I murmured:

"I'm dead, but I'm fine."

ABOUT THE AUTHOR

Elena Ferrante was born in Naples. She is the author of *The Days of Abandonment*, *Troubling Love*, and *The Lost Daughter*. Her Neapolitan novels include *My Brilliant Friend*, *The Story of a New Name*, *Those Who Leave and Those Who Stay*, and the fourth and final book in the series, *The Story of the Lost Child*.

THE NEAPOLITAN NOVELS
By Elena Ferrante

"One of modern fiction's richest portraits of a friendship."
—John Powers, *NPR's Fresh Air*

BOOK 1

"Ferrante's novels are intensely, violently personal, and because of this they seem to dangle bristling key chains of confession before the unsuspecting reader."
—James Wood, *The New Yorker*

$17.00 • 978-1-60945-078-6 • September 2012

BOOK 2

"Stunning . . . cinematic in the density of its detail."
—The *Times Literary Supplement*

$18.00 • 978-1-60945-134-9 • September 2013

BOOK 3

"Everyone should read anything with Ferrante's name on it."—Eugenia Williamson, *The Boston Globe*

$18.00 • 978-1-60945-233-9 • September 2014

"Imagine if Jane Austen got angry and you'll have some idea how explosive these works are."
—John Freeman, critic and author of *How to Read a Novelist*

The fourth and final Neapolitan novel available everywhere books are sold from **September 1 2015**.